Stain
3 - 18
AA

# STARTING FROM HERE

# STARTING

# FROM

# HERE

## Lisa Jenn Bigelow

AMAZON CHILDREN'S PUBLISHING

Text copyright © 2012 by Lisa J. Bigelow

Amazon Publishing
Attn: Marshall Cavendish Children's Books
P.O. Box 400818
Las Vegas, NV 89149
www.amazon.com/amazonchildrenspublishing

Marshall Cavendish is a trademark of Times Publishing Limited.

Library of Congress Cataloging-in-Publication Data
Bigelow, Lisa Jenn.
Starting from here / by Lisa Jenn Bigelow. — 1st ed.
p. cm.
Summary: Sixteen-year-old Colby is barely hanging on with her mother dead, her long-haul trucker father often away, her almost-girlfriend dumping her for a boy, and her failing grades, when a stray dog appears and helps her find hope.
ISBN 978-0-7614-6233-0 (hardcover) — ISBN 978-0-7614-6234-7 (ebook)
[1. Lesbians—Fiction. 2. Dating (Social customs)—Fiction. 3. Dogs—Fiction. 4. High schools—Fiction. 5. Schools—Fiction. 6. Fathers and daughters—Fiction.] I. Title.
PZ7.B4822St 2012
[Fic]—dc23
2011040129

Book design by Becky Terhune
Editor: Robin Benjamin

Printed in the United States of America (R)
First edition
10 9 8 7 6 5 4 3 2 1

In honor of my parents, Gary and Sheila,
and in memory of Carly, my four-legged muse


Special thanks to
Robin Benjamin, Lauren Boatwright,
Joe Chellman, Steven Chudney, Carey Farrell,
Faith Ferber, James Hankey, Daniel Kraus,
Kristine Rines, and Kat Stein
for feeding, grooming, and loving this stray.

**1**

**THE LAST TIME** I kissed Rachel Greenstein we lay in the bed of Scarlett, my Ford pickup, watching the sun sink beyond West Lake. It was a mild mid-November night. The branches overhead were bare, and a breeze carried the ragged scent of leaves smoking in rusty oil drums. Winter was coming, no question, but I could almost fool myself that it was summer for just one more day.

"And *poof*," Rachel said softly as the last brilliant sliver slid out of sight. "There it goes."

"Now it's just you, me, and the man in the moon," I said. "And what a dirty old man he is, spying on us girls. Pervert!" I yelled at the sky.

Rachel laughed, a low, bubbling sound.

"I can't blame him, though," I said. "It must get boring up there. Nothing to do but sit around and eat green cheese. What does green cheese taste like, anyway?"

"Blue cheese gone bad?"

"Gross. Blue cheese already tastes like it's gone bad." I cuddled closer. Rachel was a full head taller than me, but that didn't matter when we were horizontal. "So, do you think he's just a voyeur, or does he want a ménage à trois? I'd speculate, but I only got a C in astro."

Rachel didn't answer, and I felt like an idiot. Why was I running my mouth on what might be the last beautiful night of the year?

She pulled the blanket higher, enveloping us in plaid wool. Wriggling beneath, I untucked her shirt from her jeans and began kissing her belly. As my mouth moved upward, she gripped my shoulders. "Colby."

It took me a moment to realize she wasn't pulling me toward her. She was pushing me away.

"What's wrong?" I asked, resurfacing. "Chilly?"

"No, no. I just need to stop for a second." Rachel tugged down her shirt and struggled to a sitting position. She frowned out at the lake, its surface gone from sapphire to obsidian in a matter of minutes. I sat up beside her. This wasn't the first time Rachel had

2

stopped me—she'd never let me go as far as I was ready to—but we'd definitely gone farther than this.

"Rachel, come on. Talk to me."

She dug her fingers into her short, dark curls and shook her head. "I guess I'm just stressed. College apps, senior project, orchestra, the Alliance."

"It's just you and me out here. Forget that crap."

"I can't."

"Sure you can. Just lie back, close your eyes, and pretend it doesn't exist." I tucked my wispy blond hair behind my ears and leaned in, hoping for another kiss. "Trust me, it works."

"Right. I guess that's why you're failing chemistry."

I fell back, my head clunking against Scarlett's rear window. "How'd you know that?"

"Van told me."

*Van.* The only way to keep that boy's mouth shut was to wire it. "It's one lousy class," I said.

"Except it's not, is it? Van said your dad had to sign your midterm report. That's serious. And you've been in detention practically all fall."

"So I'm not the star pupil you are. I'm good at other things, right?" I squeezed her thigh, but she ignored my teasing. "Look, I'm doing fine. Maybe not your super-duper, honor roll version of 'fine,' but it's good enough for me."

"I worry about you sometimes. They say junior year's most important to colleges."

"You don't have to worry. You're not my guidance counselor, Rachel. You're my—"

*Girlfriend.* That was the word I wanted to say more than anything. But even though we'd been hanging out—making out—on and off since the summer, we'd never discussed just what we meant to each other. Every time I wanted to bring it up, I chickened out.

A strong gust blew across the lake, sending water lapping noisily onto the sand. Swallows darted in the dusky blue sky. The Michigan cold was creeping back, seeping into my butt through the corrugated metal of Scarlett's bed. I drew the blanket up to my chin. "Can we go back to making out now?"

"Colby."

My stomach knotted.

Then she said it: "I think we need to stop."

She didn't mean just for a moment. "You mean forever?" I said stupidly.

"I'm sorry."

"I don't understand. Did I do something wrong?"

"No. I mean—no."

"Did I push you too fast? Because I can lay off. It's not like I'm 100 percent hormones. Only 95." I laughed nervously.

"No! It's what I was trying to explain just now. I'm stressed. This—this thing we're doing, it—"

"I'm stressing you out?"

"No. I mean, yes. I mean, sort of." Rachel stared upward. I followed her gaze to the first glimmering stars. Then I turned back to her wide-set gray eyes, her curls that sprang back into place when I pulled them gently, the dimple in her chin that drew my fingertip like a magnet.

"I don't get it. I thought we were having fun. I thought this was, like, antistress."

"I know. And it was, for a while. But now there's so much going on in my life, and it just feels like one more thing to deal with." Rachel blinked at me. Her cheeks were wet. "It would be the same with anyone, Colby."

"But I'm not anyone," I said, even as I thought, *Am I?*

"Besides"—she sniffed and drew her sleeve under her nose—"it'll be better for you, too. I won't distract you from school—"

"I want to be distracted! For God's sake, Rachel. You're only the greatest thing I have going for me right now."

"See? This is what I'm talking about. I can't take that pressure. It's not fair to either of us to keep doing this." Her words ran laps through my head, faster and faster, until they blurred into nothing.

"Say something, Colby." Under the blanket, Rachel gripped my hand so hard my knuckles ground together.

I cleared my throat. "So, what do we do now?"

"I want to stay friends. I mean, things will be awkward at the Alliance if we don't."

"Of course. Wouldn't want things to be awkward."

She missed my sarcasm. "Right! It's not like we had a big fight or something."

I felt like throwing up.

We drove to Rachel's house in silence. "Well, um, bye," she said, stalling with the door half open. "See you at school." I nodded but didn't speak, didn't take my hands off the steering wheel. She didn't try to hug me, which was probably for the best. I don't know what I would have done.

It was only after she'd disappeared into her house and I'd put Scarlett into drive that I said what I was thinking. The words creaked out of me: "But I love you."

I made my way along the winding streets of Rachel's subdivision, then accelerated east toward the outskirts of town. I turned onto Harrington Road, passing the greenhouse and the nail salon, the animal hospital and the bait shop, the New Age place that sold crystal doodads and other items of questionable value. At last, at a break in the cornfields, I reached home, sweet home: Trail's End Mobile Home Village. I'd driven this route between Rachel's place and mine so many times these past few months. Would I ever do it again?

Our trailer was utterly still, holding its breath the way it always did when my father was away. Tonight I was grateful for the solitude. I prayed that Van wouldn't call or, worse, Dad.

I curled up on the faded blue corduroy couch and turned on the TV, but my brain wouldn't stop replaying the scene by the lake. And each time I wondered: How did I screw up? What should I have done differently so that right now I'd be lying in Rachel's arms under the stars instead of huddled in the darkness by myself? If I'd told her I loved her when I had the chance, would it have made any difference at all?

**2**

*From the Rainbow Alliance Internet Lounge:*

> **z-dawg:** Who's looking forward 2 Turkey Day? 4 DAY WEEKEND!!!
>
> **yinyang:** Isn't it kind of offensive to refer to a national holiday by the food we eat? Have some reverence!
>
> **van_the_man:** Ooo, what if we did that for all the holidays? In my family they'd all be Jell-O Salad Day!
>
> **colb33:** Or Green Bean Casserole Day. I know your mom's cooking.
>
> **kittykat96:** OK so I for one am not looking forward to this weekend because my

entire family will visit and only some of them know about me and it is a real pain in the a$$ keeping track of who knows and who doesn't and I do not want this weekend to turn into some big drama.

**yinyang:** I hear you. Most of my relatives don't even know what trans means. The last time I tried to explain, my grandmother said, "Is it like that movie Tootsie?"

**van_the_man:** I LOVE that movie. Young Dustin Hoffman in little blue jockey shorts? YUM.

**yinyang:** Um, he was like 40 . . . and so not hot . . . but you see my point.

**writergrrl:** You guys are so lucky and brave. I wish I could come out to *anyone* in my family.

**z-dawg:** Word.

• • •

Dad called from the road a couple of days before Thanksgiving. "I was really hoping to get home for the holiday this year, but it doesn't look like it's going to happen."

He hadn't made it home for Thanksgiving last year, either. In fact, I could probably count on one hand the number of years my family had sat down to eat turkey,

9

cranberry sauce, and pumpkin pie on the actual holiday. That's just part of life when you have a trucker in the family. Usually we celebrated a little early or late— except last year, when we didn't celebrate at all.

"I could call Aunt Sue," Dad said. "I'm sure she'd be happy to include you in her plans."

"No, she wouldn't. She's got a bridge game, like always. Besides, Van already asked me over. And lots of people at work are looking for subs, so I'll probably go in."

"Are you sure you'll be all right? I hate to abandon you on a holiday, Bee."

"No offense, Dad, but I'm used to it."

He sighed. "I'm making it home for Christmas, and that's a promise. I don't care if I have to pass on a job. I'm going to spend Christmas with my girl."

"Sounds good," I said, faking enthusiasm. Not that I didn't believe he meant it; I was just being realistic. "Drive safe, Dad. Love you."

When my parents had first met, Dad was a cabdriver. Mom had come to Kalamazoo for college, but she'd spent more time hanging out at the Fourth Coast Café than in her dorm, studying. Dad would stop in between fares for a cuppa. One thing led to another. Before Mom's freshman year was out, I was on the way.

Dad wasn't making enough then to support a family,

and my grandparents weren't much help. Dad's folks were scraping by on Social Security down in Florida; Mom's had pretty much disowned her when she refused to move back home and "start fresh," which to them meant give me up for adoption, go back to school, and stay far, far away from my dad. Aunt Sue, my dad's older stepsister, had helped out some. But wherever she went, her disapproval followed.

So Mom had started slinging lattes at Fourth Coast, and together, bit by bit, my parents put Dad through truck-driving school. Since I was in preschool, he'd been away for a week at a time OTR trucking: over-the-road, where the road is one of America's endless freeways. We never got rich—obviously, since we still lived in a dinky trailer—but we did okay. Mom had finished her degree, and when I hit middle school, they both had decent jobs for the first time in my life.

And then Mom had gotten her diagnosis.

When she died a year and a half ago, folks had said to my dad, "You're going to work closer to home now, aren't you, Bob? What about Colby?" But given the economy, cabdriving was less reliable than ever, and short-haul jobs were hard to come by. So Dad had gone back on the road.

At first I'd stayed with Aunt Sue in her one-bedroom condo across town. That was a bust. It had been tolerable

11

during Mom's stints in the hospital, but only because I'd known it was temporary. When Aunt Sue had gotten after me about my "lack of commitment" to schoolwork, scolding me that my parents deserved better, I'd kept my mouth shut and made a show of trying harder. If Mom could deal with radiation and chemotherapy, I could deal with Aunt Sue.

It was different after Mom died. I was sick of being under house arrest until every speck of homework satisfied Aunt Sue. I was sick of sleeping on her foldaway couch with its springs poking my back and dust mites making me sneeze. I was sick of pretending to be grateful when I longed to escape. There was no way I could make it three years until graduation and freedom.

After I'd run away from Sue's for the fifth time, Dad figured it was safer for me to stay home or at Van's than to walk across town and down Harrington Road at three in the morning. That's when we'd made our cell phone pact: I was required to keep my phone charged and at the ready, night or day. Outside of school or work, I had to answer it, even if I didn't recognize the number on the caller ID. It might be Dad trying to reach me from somewhere on the road—or someone trying to reach me for him.

The truth was, I didn't expect much from Dad anymore. He loved me, I knew, and had worked hard to provide for me over the years. But for every day I saw him, there were seven days I didn't. Fifty years could pass, and I wouldn't get half as close to him as I'd been to Mom. I'd never even told him about Rachel and me.

• • •

On Thanksgiving I put in eight hours of bagging Potato Buds and Stove Top at Meijer Thrifty Acres—not a bad deal, considering the holiday pay. Most of my money went toward Scarlett, Dad's gift for my sixteenth birthday. I'd been all set to call her the Red Death—we'd been reading Poe in English class—but Dad insisted I'd see better results if I treated her like a lady, so Miss Scarlett O'Hara it was. She was in pretty good shape considering her age, but there was insurance to pay, and she was a terrible gas-guzzler. She was totally worth it, though. Without her I would have been stranded at Trail's End.

After work I drove to Van's house, half a mile south of mine. He, his mom, and his twenty-year-old sister, Danielle, had moved from the other side of town after his parents' divorce when Van and I were in sixth grade. Compared to our trailer, their house was the Ramada. It had powder-blue vinyl siding, plush carpeting, three bedrooms, and an extra half bathroom in Mrs. McIneany's room.

Mrs. McIneany greeted me at the door with a quick hug. "Make yourself at home, Colby. The turkey's in the roaster, and Van's Tofurky is in the oven. Knock on wood, we'll have dinner on the table in half an hour."

I held out the foil-topped bottle of sparkling cider I'd picked up at work. "Smells great. Is there anything I can do to help?"

"Nope. Danielle's in the kitchen with me, and we're knocking elbows as it is. Go ahead and find Van. I think he's in his room keeping Teddy occupied."

The McIneanys' smash-nosed Himalayan cat, Precious, gave me her usual friendly hiss as I slid out of my sneakers. I padded to Van's room, where I found him sprawled on the floor with a heap of building blocks and his nephew, Teddy.

Teddy was not quite two and really cute, with the same sandy-brown hair as Van, though Teddy's curled wildly at his collar while Van kept his buzzed. Teddy began babbling unintelligibly when he saw me.

Van translated. "Yes, that's right! Colby's here for Thanksgiving, too!"

I lowered myself to the carpet with a groan. "Long day?" Van asked.

"Is there any other kind?" I rubbed the heels of my hands into my eyes. "If you told me an asteroid was about to hit Earth and kill everybody, including me, I think I would finally have something to be thankful for."

"Wow, dramatic much?" Van said. "Look, if this is about Rachel—"

"What would possibly give you that idea?"

"—you have got to stop. Are you going to let her haunt you forever? Because that is just not healthy."

"It hasn't been forever. It's been a week. And I can't help it, Van. She dumped me for no reason."

"I thought she said she was stressed out."

"That wasn't the real reason. How could that be the real reason? There must be something else, something she didn't want to tell me."

"Does it matter?" Van asked. "It's over now."

"But if there was something I could change . . . if she'd give me another chance—" A sob caught in my throat. Teddy's head swiveled, a puzzled look on his chubby face.

"Aw, Colby," Van said, scooting over and putting an arm around me. "Forget her. She's not worth it."

I sniffled. "You know that's not true."

Rachel was special. From the moment I'd met her at an Alliance meeting my sophomore year, something about her had gotten to me. She was so cute, without having any idea. Kind and smart, too. Van had agreed, and we started inviting her along when we went to the movies or the mall or the park.

It didn't hurt that she was something of a mystery. Van and I had played the "Is she or isn't she?" game for months. Her short hair and tomboy fashion sense screamed queer, but to the best of our knowledge, she'd never gone out with anyone. I'd lie awake at night aching to find out.

The first time Rachel and I kissed had been a summer afternoon. The three of us were supposed to meet at Milham Park to kick around my old soccer ball. I hadn't played a real game since Mom died and I quit the Lady Wolves, but I still had my gear, and I liked to get outside and run after the ball, to send it sailing over the grass. It made me feel powerful.

That day Van had bailed at the last minute, and I decided to act. Before I left home I brushed my teeth for a good five minutes. Then, on my way to the park, I got so nervous I snarfed half a bag of stale sour cream–and–onion potato chips from Scarlett's glove box. I'd stopped at a drug store and picked up some candy to get rid of the taste. When I finally kissed Rachel, my mouth tasted like raspberries and cream. Before long, hers had, too.

Van sighed. "I like Rachel. I do. But she hurt you, and that means she's on my shit list."

I snorted. "Yeah, right, your shit list. So next time you see her you'll give her the stink eye and *then* give her a hug?"

"All right, you've got me there." Van pressed his lips to my forehead. "But you'll always be my special-est friend. You know that."

"Until you get a boyfriend."

"Even then, may it happen in this lifetime." Van put his hand over his heart. "Semper fidelis."

I wiped my eyes. "The marines *so* don't want you. You realize that, right?"

"Of course they do. They just don't know it yet. Give me five years, and I'll be changing diapers in Afghanistan and building skate parks in Burundi."

"I think you're confusing the Marine Corps with the Peace Corps."

"But I've already got the haircut!" Van ran his hand over his buzz. "And I'd love to wear one of those funny little hats. *Ooo, ooo!* Do you think the turkey's done? I can show you my prowess with a blade!"

I laughed and shook my head. I didn't know how I'd survive without Van.

• • •

I returned to school Monday determined to show Rachel that heartbreak wouldn't get the best of me. I still loved her, and my heart hurt like hell, but I'd respect her decision. I'd be her friend, her completely platonic friend. And maybe once her life settled down she'd realize how much she missed me, and things would go back to the way they were—except this time we'd officially be a couple.

Between first and second periods, I caught a glimpse of her in the hallway. I opened my mouth to call her name. But I stopped—at first because I wasn't sure it was Rachel after all, and then because I was.

Rachel Greenstein was walking the halls of Westnedge High holding hands with a boy.

**3**

**H**IS NAME WAS Michael Schmidt. I had to wait an agonizing two hours until lunch period to learn this, and then it was all my friends would talk about. Michael was a senior like Rachel. He was on the honor roll like Rachel. He was Jewish like Rachel. He was even tall like Rachel.

"They must've had some weekend," Zak said. We looked across the cafeteria to where they sat with a bunch of Michael's friends. Even last week when it had killed me to sit so close to her, Rachel had kept having lunch with us. "They're all over each other. I wonder what was in that gravy, if you know what I'm saying."

"Dude, shut up," said Van, tipping his head in my direction. Rachel and I might never have been

19

official, but everyone in the Alliance knew there'd been something between us.

"Oh. Sorry," Zak said. "This shit really blows." He paused. "So, does this mean Rachel's bi? Or is she straight, and Colby was just a—what do you call it—anomaly?"

"Dude!"

I watched Michael grasp Rachel's shoulder as they laughed about something. I longed to march over there, rip his paws off her, and kick him in the part of his anatomy that *wasn't* like Rachel.

"I, for one, am disgusted," Liliana said. "Look at her, totally flaunting it." Liliana sidled in close and slipped her arm around my waist. "You know, Colby, you shouldn't let her bring you down. You've got to show her you're still in the game."

Zak smirked. "You think making out with you is going to improve Colby's mood? Think again, girlfriend."

"Why not? It's worked before." Liliana pressed her cheek against my shoulder. "Besides, I didn't say it had to be me! But it *could* be. Just to show Rachel."

Liliana's perfume smelled like apple pie with too much sugar. I shoved my uneaten sandwich across the table and stood up. "I've got to go."

Grabbing my backpack, I rushed down the deserted back hall, past the automotive and wood shops, and out into the clammy, gray cold.

Van caught up less than a minute later, panting. "Sorry about those idiots."

"It's not your fault." I hugged myself, shivering. I didn't smoke, but right then I wanted a cigarette. It might have helped to warm me up and given an excuse for the ache in my chest. When I came to school that morning, I'd thought the worst was over. *Wrong.*

"Zak's a bonehead. And Liliana—"

"Will flirt with anyone with boobs? I know, Van. It's not them."

"I know. Hey, you're cold." He yanked his hoodie over his head and pushed it into my arms.

I clutched it to my stomach. "She lied to me. She said it wasn't me, that it would be the same with anyone, but now she's with him."

"Put on the sweatshirt, Col. There's no sense in both of us freezing."

I pulled it over my head. It held the faint scent of lemon laundry detergent mixed with the pizza and peanut butter of the cafeteria and a hint of boy sweat. I immediately felt warmer but couldn't stop shaking. "You know what the worst thing is?" I asked through chattering teeth.

Van stepped close and rubbed my arms. Goose bumps stood out on his pale forearms. "What?"

"It's the way they were touching and didn't even care who saw them. The way they were holding hands.

21

We were together almost *five months*. She never let me touch her when anyone else was around, except you."

"Oh, Col. You know how some people are."

"But everyone knows Rachel's in the Alliance. What did she have to lose?"

I remembered meeting Rachel's parents. I'd stood in their living room, surrounded by paintings bigger than I was—paintings you could tell were the real deal. I'd tried not to stare down at my dingy socks.

Rachel and I had been hooking up for a couple of months by then, and I was already in way over my head. I'd thought maybe, just *maybe*—but when Rachel introduced me, it was "Mom, Dad, this is my friend Colby from school." *Friend.*

As they smiled and shook my hand, I'd felt myself fade. It took being alone with Rachel, feeling her lips against mine again, hearing her breath, to bring me back.

Maybe Rachel had already known things wouldn't last long between us. Maybe she'd already decided she didn't want me, and it was only a matter of time before she found someone better to replace me. Maybe that was why I'd never told Rachel how I felt. I'd known what she would say—or wouldn't.

Van grasped my hand. "Come back inside. Lunch is almost over."

I let him drag me in, but I had no idea how I could

get through another three hours of school knowing that somewhere in the building Rachel was daydreaming about Michael Schmidt.

"You could talk to Mr. P.," Van said. Mr. Peabody was the only "out" teacher at Westnedge High and the Alliance's faculty adviser. "I'm sure he'd have some advice."

"That would be weird. He sees Rachel all the time."

"Yeah, I guess you're right."

We plodded out of the tech wing, skirting the hall monitors and ducking upstairs to our lockers. "Hey," Van said, "what do you call a cow that won't give milk?"

I sighed. "I don't know."

"A Milk Dud!"

No response.

"Come on, Col, you've got to admit it's funny."

"No, I don't."

"Not even a little bit?"

I forced a smile, but it was more like a grimace. I didn't want to talk to Mr. Peabody. I didn't want to hear Van's corny jokes. There was only one person I wanted right now—to bury my face in her neck and cry until I couldn't cry anymore, to have her tell me everything was going to be okay—and she'd been dead for a year and a half.

**4**

*From the Rainbow Alliance Internet Lounge:*

> **stonebutterfly:** Did anyone go to the Snow-flake Semiformal?
>
> **z-dawg:** Are you for serious? N to the O. Not after the Spring Fling.
>
> **stonebutterfly:** What happened?
>
> **van_the_man:** Zak and I were dancing. It wasn't a slow song. We weren't even touching. But afterward I mysteriously got slammed against a wall. I swear I have brick-shaped scars.
>
> **z-dawg:** They didn't touch me but on

Monday I found "fag" written all over my locker. Again.

**kittykat96:** Well I for one had an amazing time at Snowflake. I danced with EVERYONE, boy or girl, and no one said a thing.

**yinyang:** Don't forget me!

**kittykat96:** That's right, I also danced with my favorite two-spirited friend. :-)

**writergrrl:** Maybe no one said anything to *you* but that doesn't mean they weren't talking.

**kittykat96:** How do you know? I didn't see you there.

**writergrrl:** I was serving punch. Trust me, you can learn a lot serving punch.

**van_the_man:** Oooooo, give us some dirt!

**writergrrl:** No way! I'm a journalist, not Perez Hilton.

**van_the_man:** Well, P to the O-O on you. I'll just take my enquiring mind elsewhere.

• • •

The day before winter break I left chemistry class with the certainty that I'd failed yet another test. The night before I'd stayed up past midnight, trying to make sense of acids and bases until my eyes were as red as the numbers on the clock. But when the bell rang, my exam was still half blank.

"Happy holidays!" Mrs. Hoekstra said as she collected my test.

I just walked out.

In the hall I darted around gaggles of girls squealing and hugging as if they were leaving on a mission to Mars instead of going home to cookies and eggnog. I sidestepped jocks twice my size and slipped into the stairwell, only to get an eyeful of tongue wrestling—all boy-girl, of course. I wanted to escape, the faster and farther away the better, but my coat and keys were still in my locker.

I was twenty feet from my locker when a Frisbee whizzed toward my head. A tall, balding figure stepped out of a doorway and grabbed it before it clocked me.

"*Colby* Bingham!" Mr. Peabody beamed down at me. "Where have you been hiding?"

"Oh, I, uh—"

I hadn't been to an Alliance meeting since Rachel and Michael started going out. In a school of two thousand, it wasn't that hard to avoid her. All I had to do was reroute my paths between classes, sit with my back to her new lunch table, limit contact with our mutual friends, and stop attending my favorite club. See? Easy. I still dropped in on the Alliance's "Internet Lounge," but only because I didn't have to look Rachel in the eye there.

"The Alliance is heading over to Fazoli's," Mr. Peabody said. "What better way to say farewell to fall than with a bottomless basket of breadsticks?"

My mouth watered at the thought, but I said, "Sorry, Mr. P., I really need to get home."

I pushed onward—then regretted it. Rachel was leaning beside my locker.

"Colby. You're avoiding me."

I opened my locker and dropped my chemistry book inside. *Bang.* "What gave you that idea?"

"I thought we were going to try to stay friends."

"And I thought you were too stressed out to see anyone. At least, that's what someone told me. Guess they were wrong. Or flat-out lying."

She ignored the jab. "A bunch of us are going to Fazoli's. Want to come?"

"It depends." I pulled on my coat and patted the pockets for my keys. "Is *he* coming?"

"He doesn't have to," Rachel said. "I told him it might be too soon."

"So you're saying it's up to me?"

"Well, yeah. I don't want to make you uncomfortable."

"How sweet. So if I say no, there's no question

who the big, fat jerk is."

"Come on, Colby. I don't want to fight."

"Of course not. Why fight when it's so easy to get your way? 'Oh, it's not the right time for me to be with anyone.' Anyone except Michael Schmidt!" I couldn't stop now. "Did I disgust you from the beginning? Did you think you were doing me a favor? The whole time, did you secretly wish you were with a guy?"

"Colby, stop it! I wasn't ready, okay? I got scared."

"Why do I get the feeling you'd never be ready for me?" I folded my arms and stared her down. The hallways weren't exactly empty yet, and I wasn't exactly being discreet. But I didn't care. Anyone who didn't already know I was gay was welcome to find out now. I was used to name-calling and dirty looks from the homophobes of Westnedge High. It would take a lot more than that to shut me up.

After a long moment Rachel sighed. "I'm not going to lie. Some things are easier with Michael."

"No kidding. Because now you can give your mom that nice, Jewish wedding and have lots of babies and forget all about your 'experiment' with me—"

"Colby—"

"I should have known from the start I was wasting my time. You can't change a straight girl."

"I'm not straight. I—I don't know what I am. But I didn't fake a thing with you."

I remembered the way Rachel's fingers had tangled in my hair when she kissed me, and I believed her. I swallowed the rest of my angry words. The lump in my throat was as hard as a peach pit.

"About Fazoli's," Rachel said. "I'll tell Michael it's not the right time."

"No, it's okay. I already told Mr. P. that I wasn't going."

"Well, maybe you and I could hang out over break. See a movie or go ice-skating."

I should have told her no. Why torture myself? But instead I said, "Maybe."

Maybe if I gave Rachel time, she'd realize how much she'd given up.

"All right. I'll call you. We'll figure something out," she said.

Rachel opened her arms to hug me, but I pretended to see something else I needed from my locker and turned away. She got the hint and stepped back, back to the arms of her new boyfriend and a bottomless basket of breadsticks.

I found Van down the hall, strapping his skateboard to the bottom of the purple, paisley tote bag he'd made in home ec. He broke into his chip-toothed grin when he saw me. "Are you working this afternoon? Did you hear about Fazoli's?"

I groaned and banged my forehead against the nearest locker.

"I'll take that as a yes." Van stood and pulled a puffy, green vest over his hoodie. "Come on, it'll be fun."

"Not with You-Know-Who there."

Van giggled. "You make him sound like Voldemort."

"He might as well be."

"You can sit at opposite ends of the—"

"No, Van. I'm just— It's too— I can't. Not yet."

Van shifted from foot to foot. "Well, I'd ride home with you, but I already told Mr. P.—"

"It's fine. Really. Just give me a call when you get home, okay?"

"Sure." He loped off toward Mr. Peabody's room. I headed for the door.

The sky was gloomy with clouds and freezing drizzle. Scarlett was a beacon in the gray parking lot. I fired her up, turned on the wipers, and joined the line of cars waiting to get out of the lot. The engine almost drowned out the growling of my stomach.

The Alliance kids frolicked down the sidewalk toward Fazoli's. Van walked beside Mr. Peabody, his paisley tote and skateboard swinging at his side. Near the head of the pack, Michael Schmidt carried a huge, orange Westnedge High golf umbrella. Rachel held his arm. It was very sweet. So sweet it made my stomach hurt.

## 5

**PARKED IN THE MUD** beside our trailer. It was a yellowed, vintage single-wide with only four rooms (if you counted the bathroom). There was a bedroom on either end, and in the middle was the living room with its kitchen alcove. It wasn't much, but it was plenty big enough for Dad and me, especially considering how little Dad was home.

On my way in I grabbed the mail and sorted out the bills from the junk. I didn't bother opening the Christmas cards in their red and green envelopes. I knew they'd say "Merry Xmas, Bob and Colby!" and "All best for the new year, Bob and Colby!" as if Mom never existed. I left them in a tidy stack on the table for Dad. He wasn't due to arrive home until Christmas

Eve, and I wasn't convinced he'd make it.

I nuked a frozen ham and cheese pocket, trying not to imagine the thick, steaming slice of lasagna I could have had at Fazoli's. I pictured Rachel and Michael cozied up at the restaurant, feeding each other forkfuls of rigatoni, surrounded by friends—*my* friends—and felt sick.

I gobbled my food as I ran a feather duster over the coffee table, the TV, the bookshelves crammed with Dad's travel books, the garage sale paintings of desert sunsets and misty mountain lakes. I dragged out the Dirt Devil and used the brush attachment to suck up all the crumbs from the couch. I washed the dishes and set them in the rack to dry, gave the toilet a halfhearted scrub, and took a look around.

The place looked decent, but it didn't look the slightest bit Christmassy.

So I tuned the radio to a station that played Christmas music 24/7. I unearthed our little artificial tree from Dad's closet and set it on the coffee table. I scattered some old tinsel across the branches and hooked on some shiny balls and the crusty, misshapen clay ornaments I'd made in preschool. They used to embarrass me, but Mom would never let me throw them out. I wasn't about to go against her wishes now. We used to have an angel for the top of the tree, but I couldn't find it. In its place I put a mini rubber chicken that Van had once given me as a gag gift.

Finally, I unpacked the pair of porcelain turtledoves. They'd been one of my parents' wedding gifts—from Dad's parents, of course; Mom's had been in denial. I carefully wiped the dust from the doves and hung them in the very center of the tree, facing the couch.

Mom and I used to string popcorn and cranberries for garlands, which we'd hang outside for the birds when Christmas was over. We'd cut paper snowflakes for the windows. She always roasted a turkey and made five different kinds of cookies. My favorites were peanut butter with a Hershey's Kiss pressed into the center.

Nowadays Dad and I ordered a ready-to-eat dinner from Meijer: turkey breast with all the trimmings, green beans, and pecan pie. It was good food, but you know how people say Christmas doesn't come in a box? That goes double for the microwave.

When there wasn't anything more I could do to summon the Christmas spirit, I collapsed on the couch to wait for Van's call. As John Denver crooned me to sleep, singing of peace on Earth and goodwill toward men, the rain slowly turned to snow.

• • •

My phone jolted me awake. Van.

"What's orange and sounds like a parrot?"

I groaned. "Can we cut to the chase?"

"A carrot! Isn't that great? Mr. P. told it at Fazoli's."

"Knee slapping."

"Well, somebody's wearing their crabby pants. Come on, Col, we've got two weeks' vacation. Time to quit moping and get out of the house."

"But I've almost perfected my technique."

"Don't make me break out the Bing Crosby. 'You've got to ac-cent-uate the positive—'"

"Okay, okay. I'll get out of the house," I said. "What's your grand plan? I'll tell you now, I'm not driving you to the mall. It'll be a mob scene."

"Actually"—Van's voice took on a guilty tone—"I was hoping you'd help me collect cans."

"Wow, you sure do know how to entertain a lady."

"I know, I'm sorry. But I haven't done my Christmas shopping yet, and I could really use the cash."

For all the Teddy-sitting Van did, he didn't make a cent. He supplemented his allowance with the deposits on pop and beer cans he found along Harrington Road—which, given the amount of litter people tossed out their car windows, wasn't too shabby an enterprise. Sometimes he roped me into helping.

"It's all right," I said. "It's not as if I have anything better to do."

"And we could go back to my place after," Van said.

34

"I've got stuff for making brownies. Well, except for eggs. Eggs aren't that important, are they?" he asked hopefully.

I shuffled to the fridge and peered inside. "I can bring eggs." One good thing about working at a grocery store: no excuse for a bare fridge.

"Fantastic. In that case, meet you halfway?"

I pulled on my sneakers and winter coat and hat, all of which had started out as my favorite color, baby pink, but were well on their way to pussy willow gray. I slipped two eggs into one pocket and my toothbrush into the other, in case I ended up spending the night at Van's. I grabbed a big, black garbage bag from under the kitchen sink.

Outside, specks of snow skittered by. The sun, after barely showing its face all day, sagged in the sky. Car exhaust hung in the damp air. I trudged down the drive, past the rows of trailers and the chipped and battered Trail's End sign, run into so many times by drunk drivers that no one bothered to count anymore.

On the shoulder of Harrington Road, broken glass and gravel crunched under my feet. Van and I called this stretch "Roadkill Road" because we always had to sidestep at least one dead cat, possum, raccoon, or squirrel—sometimes even a deer. The speeding cars sent wind whipping through my hair and sprayed pebbles against my shins. Whenever I spied a metallic glint, I stooped to investigate and, if I was lucky, added a squashed can to my bag. After I met up with Van, we'd comb the weeds more thoroughly.

I saw Van coming up on the far side of the road, a garbage bag of his own swinging by his ankles. When we were directly opposite each other, he looked both ways and slouched across the street. "Pickings are slim," he said. "Think Danielle will mind if I do her shopping at the dollar store? Their perfume can't be any worse than the stuff she usually wears." He looked past me and blinked. "Hey, who's your stalker?"

"Ha, ha," I said, not in the mood for another corny joke.

"No, seriously, check it out."

I turned. At first I thought the flash of white among the weeds was just an old newspaper tumbling toward us, or maybe a plastic bag. But as it came nearer, I saw it was a dog: a big, white dog with black, folded ears and a black patch over one eye. He paused among the dead thistles and broken beer bottles and wadded-up trash, staring at us. As we stared back, his tail began to swish.

"For a stalker, he's pretty darn cute," Van said.

"It's not a Trail's End dog," I said. "Do you recognize it from down your way?"

"Nope. Doesn't look like he's got a collar, either."

"People are so dumb. Who lets their dog run loose on Harrington Road? One wrong move and he's toast."

"I bet he's a stray," Van said. "Look how skinny he is. I'd take him home and feed him if it weren't for Precious."

"I'd take him home and feed him if Dad didn't hate dogs."

"Oh, come on. Your dad doesn't hate dogs."

"Okay, but he's never let me have one, has he?" Dad always said we didn't have the time, money, or space for a pet. Worse, he was right.

I squatted and snapped my fingers. "Here, boy! Away from the road! You idiot."

The dog didn't move.

"Wow, you could be the next Dog Whisperer," Van said.

"Shut up." I felt in my pockets, hoping a stick of beef jerky or a package of cheese crackers had magically appeared. Just the eggs. "Got any snacks?" I asked Van.

"Nope. We'll just have to turn on the charm."

"Well, help me out here, Prince Charming."

Van crouched beside me. We slapped our thighs and whistled and called to the dog in the most cutesy-ootsy voices we could muster. He only watched us with polite interest until, at last, he picked his way forward through the brush.

"That's right!" I held out my hands for him to inspect. His cold nose whiffled across my fingers, whiskers tickling my palms. The sniffing turned to licking, and I laughed. "He sure is friendly."

Van scratched him behind the ears. "He sure stinks."

"He's a hobo. What do you expect?" I dug my fingernails into the dog's barrel chest and scratched away. His black-spotted fur was caked with dirt and, for all I knew, fleas, but he enjoyed it. He sank to his hindquarters, one foot thumping against the hard ground.

I imagined coming home to his wagging tail instead of to a stale, empty trailer. Curling up on the couch with him, watching TV or reading. Taking him for long walks by the lake. Driving around in Scarlett, his boxy head hanging out the window, tongue lolling. Sharing a pillow with him on shivery nights when the only sound was my own breathing, the neighbors' TVs, and the cars on Harrington Road.

After he'd had a bath, of course. "I wish I *could* take him home," I told Van. "I kind of love him already."

"Maybe we could take him to your place, just for a couple of hours. It would get him off the street for a while."

"And then what?"

"Um. We call the police? Maybe someone's reported him missing."

"We don't have a leash."

"He seems to like us. I bet he'd follow if we started walking."

It was worth a try, but as we stood, the dog scrambled back.

"Okay, so he's a little jumpy," Van said with a laugh.

"Hey, boy! Over here. This way." I clapped my hands, but the dog hung back. "It's getting dark. He's going to get creamed if he stays out here."

"Keep walking," Van said. "That's what I do when it's time to leave the playground and Teddy won't come. I walk a little ways, and in no time he's screaming my name and running to catch up."

We started slowly toward Trail's End. I kept a lookout over my shoulder, but the dog still didn't follow. He grew smaller and smaller, a pale blotch in the growing gloom.

"What's wrong with him?" I said. "We were his best friends a minute ago."

"Dunno. Maybe he's been hurt. You know, like, gun-shy. Except without the gun. Hopefully."

The idea that anyone would raise a hand against this sweet, friendly dog infuriated me. "We can't leave him now. I'm going back."

"Are you sure that's—" Van began, but I was already running. If I could just grab the dog by the scruff of the neck, soon we'd be home, and I'd open up a can of corned beef hash for him. It would probably be the best dinner he'd had in days, maybe longer.

Too late I realized my mistake. The dog shied away again, off the shoulder and into the road, oblivious of the cars. I screamed, "No! Get back here, you stupid dog!"

But he didn't, not in time. There was a sickening whack, and the dog was lying on the ground at my feet.

**6**

**T**HERE WAS NO SCREECH of tires. The car that hit him barely slowed down, speeding off into the falling snow before I even thought to look at its license plate. Nobody else stopped, either.

I fell on my knees, sobbing, gravel and broken glass digging through my jeans. The dog's chest heaved as he struggled to get up, but I could see he wouldn't be running anywhere. His right hind leg was a wreck. Bones splintered through the skin. Blood seeped into the ground around him.

"Van, what do we do?"

"Give me your keys." Van grabbed them and sprinted in the direction of Trail's End.

I stroked the dog's head but drew back when he

growled. "It's okay," I whispered. "Hang in there. We'll get you help. You'll be fine." His eyes were wide and panicked. He didn't believe it any more than I did.

I knew I had to put pressure on the wound with a clean cloth. But his leg was such a mess, I didn't know where to start. I slipped off one of my shoes, then my sock. Ignoring the dog's growling, I knotted my sock around his bad leg.

"*Shh,*" I said. "I'm sorry. I'm so, so sorry."

I was just retying my shoe when tires crunched on the shoulder. Van pulled past us, facing the wrong way. Cars swerved, horns blaring. An almost-dead dog and two teenagers were easy to ignore; Scarlett was not. Van leapt out, leaving the motor running and the headlights glowing through the gloom. He carried my plaid star-watching blanket. I hadn't used it since my last night with Rachel.

Van spread the blanket on the ground. Wiping my nose and eyes with the back of my hand, I helped slide the dog awkwardly onto the blanket. He yelped and jerked. "Easy, boy," Van said, pressing him to the ground. "You're half roadkill already."

Van lowered Scarlett's tailgate, and we lifted the blanket like a hammock. It took all my strength to keep my end up, but we did it. The dog lay motionless in the back of the truck, too weak to struggle anymore.

"You drive," I told Van.

If these were the dog's final moments, I didn't want him to spend them alone. I'd gotten him into this mess; I wasn't about to abandon him now. I scrambled up beside him. Van slammed the tailgate, hopped into the cab, and threw Scarlett into gear. Her tires screeched as Van did a U-ey and made for the animal hospital up Harrington Road.

I blocked out the chill wind and bumpy road and snow settling on my shoulders, putting all my concentration into a prayer to Baby Jesus or Allah or whatever god or goddess would stop and listen: *Please don't take him.* I remembered sitting at Mom's bedside as she slept through her last few days, swearing to myself she'd get better, even though the doctors said it was just a matter of time. Prayer hadn't worked then. Why should it now?

The dog whined feebly as if to say, *I'm still here.*

We squealed into the clinic parking lot, nearly empty of cars. Barking dogs greeted us from somewhere beyond the two-story, white clapboard building. The driver door squeaked open, then slammed shut. Van's pale face peeked over the side. "You okay?"

"Yeah. And he—he's holding on."

"Hang tight. I'll get help."

"It won't be long now, buddy," I whispered into the dog's crumpled black ear.

A minute later I heard quick footsteps crunching across the gravel and voices: Van's, high and worried, and a woman's, so calm and cheerful that I wondered if I was hearing her right. Then Van lowered the tailgate, and there was a face to go with her voice. She was a middle-aged, auburn-haired woman in a white lab coat. "Let's see about getting this fella inside," she said.

A second woman with braided black hair stepped into view. She wore blue scrubs and carried a stretcher under her arm. I ducked out of the way as the two women climbed into Scarlett's bed. They murmured between them. "Shallow breathing . . . accelerated heart rate . . . dilated pupils . . . pale gums . . ."

On the count of three they slid their hands under the dog's hips and shoulders and pulled him onto the stretcher. The woman in blue folded my blanket into a thick pad and slid it under the dog's hindquarters. The two climbed briskly down, the stretcher between them. Van held open the clinic's door, and we followed them through the empty waiting room and down the hall to a room at the end.

The room was painted a soft, ferny green. Van and I hovered as the women laid the dog on the stainless steel table, his butt still propped up by my now-filthy blanket.

"I'm Dr. Robyn Voorhees, by the way," said the

white-coated woman as she examined the dog. "And this is Cindy Elwin, my technician." The other woman smiled briefly. "And who's this?" She nodded at the dog.

My heart skipped. What would she say if she knew the truth? *Work on a stray? Not worth my time. Call the pound. I don't want him bleeding all over my pretty office.*

"We don't—" Van began, but I stepped on his foot and glared him into silence.

"Mo," I said. "My dog's name is Mo. And I'm Colby Bingham."

"Donovan McIneany," Van said, wincing, "but call me Van."

"Well, Colby and Van," Dr. Voorhees said, stepping away from the table, "the good news is that Mo is going to pull through."

I pride myself on not being a squealer, but I squealed at that moment and burst into tears. Van hugged me and rubbed my back.

Dr. Voorhees continued. "Mo's showing signs of shock, which is why we've raised his bottom—to get blood flowing to his head. But his vitals have already grown stronger in the time he's been here." She smiled at our blank stares. "That's a very good thing."

Van cleared his throat. "So, the bad news?"

"Well, obviously, Mo has been seriously injured.

Just how seriously, I won't know until we've done X-rays. I've very concerned about that hind leg. It's not hemorrhaging, thanks to the tourniquet you made. But it's in bad shape. I wouldn't be surprised to find some fractured ribs, too, but it's that back leg—

"Listen, why don't you two wash up and fill out Mo's paperwork while Cindy and I finish our examination? I already sent my receptionist home for the day, so I'll get the forms for you."

Cindy stayed with Mo while Van and I followed Dr. Voorhees. "The bathroom's here," she said, flipping the light switch in a small, rose-colored room that looked like it belonged in somebody's house, not an animal hospital. There was even a frilly curtain around an old claw-foot tub. "I'll leave the paperwork in the reception area. Answer the questions as best you can. By the way, do you want to call your parents?"

"My dad's working," I said quickly. I couldn't let Dad blow Mo's cover.

Dr. Voorhees frowned. "Can't he be bothered in an emergency?"

"No. He's out of state and won't be home till Christmas Eve." I clenched my jaw. "Anyway, I'm sixteen. Almost seventeen. And Mo's mine. I make all decisions for him."

"But maybe your mother?"

"She's busy, too," I said. "Being dead." Best conversation stopper ever.

Sure enough, she gave up. "I'm sorry. I'll just leave the forms."

In the bathroom I noticed the dark blood crusted under my fingernails and in the creases of my knuckles. As I scrubbed, I caught a glimpse of myself in the mirror. I was a mess, my blond hair so straggly I looked like a scarecrow losing its stuffing.

The waiting room was painted the cheery color of lemon pudding. A red-bowed evergreen wreath filled the air with its piney scent. While Van washed up, I sat on a wooden bench and picked up the clipboard holding the forms. My name, address, and phone number—easy. Pet's name: Mo. Species: dog. Sex: male. Duh.

Then it got harder. Breed? I wrote *mutt*. Age? No clue. *Four* seemed like a happy medium. When did he last get his shots? How often did a dog get shots, anyway?

The bench creaked as Van sat beside me. "What's wrong?"

"I don't know the answers to most of these questions."

"She said just do your best, right?"

"No—I mean, yes, she did, but—don't you get it? She'll know." I lowered my voice. "She'll know Mo's not really my dog."

"He's yours now, right? You said so yourself. I have the sore foot to prove it."

"Yeah, but—"

"Why should it matter whether you've had him half an hour or half a year?"

"Forget it. Just help me make this shit up."

We were nearly finished when Dr. Voorhees returned. "Mo's being a very good boy. Very calm."

"The X-rays?" I asked. "Did you do them?"

She nodded. "Mo is basically a miracle. Aside from a couple of hairline fractures in the rib cage, he's all right. Except that hind leg . . . It's shattered beyond repair." She rubbed her chin. "Breaks this bad don't ever heal perfectly. It might take multiple surgeries to put it back together, and even then it won't be right. Not to mention the risk of infection and other complications. He might drag the leg around for the rest of his life, and it would likely cause him a lot of pain."

"What does that mean?" I asked. "It doesn't mean— Isn't there anything— Are you just going to—"

Dr. Voorhees touched my arm. "Dogs are strong creatures, Colby. They're very good at overcoming obstacles. What I'm suggesting is amputation. After that, chances are Mo would be getting around like before in a matter of days."

I didn't know whether to be relieved or horrified. I imagined Dr. Voorhees striding toward Mo with an ax, raising it high, and swinging it down on his leg. My stomach wrenched. Van squeezed my hand.

"Before you decide," Dr. Voorhees said, "let me tell you more about the procedure."

She rattled on about anesthetic and antibiotics and "taking" the leg below Mo's hip. After a couple hours of surgery and a day's rest at the clinic, Mo would be ready to go home. There was no mention of an ax. At last she stopped talking and looked at me expectantly.

I swallowed. "Do you give him a replacement leg? Like a war vet?"

"Or a pirate?" Van said. "You know, a doggy peg leg? *Arrrrrf.*"

Dr. Voorhees smiled and shook her head. "No prosthetic. He won't need one. Believe it or not, most dogs don't even realize they're missing a leg."

I looked at Van helplessly, but he said, "It's your decision, Col."

I closed my eyes and saw Mo, this dog who'd just slammed into my life and whose future was now in my hands. Then I opened my eyes and saw Dr. Voorhees watching me quietly. I didn't believe she'd suggest this if it weren't Mo's best option.

"I guess three legs are better than nothing," I said. "Let's do it."

Dr. Voorhees nodded. "It's late in the day, and I'd like to look at Mo with a fresh pair of eyes in the morning. We can keep him here overnight, keep his pain under control, do the surgery first thing, and still have him home in time for Christmas."

She paused. Her gaze dropped to my ratty sneakers, then traveled up to my shabby coat before meeting my eyes once more. She knew.

I waited.

She said, "Seeing as you're a minor, I really should talk to your father before going beyond immediate first aid."

"Mo's my dog, not his! I told you, I make the decisions."

"And pay the bills? Amputation is an expensive surgery."

"Yeah." I rose to my feet. "I have a job. Just tell me how much it is. I'll pay for it."

"It runs about a thousand dollars."

I fell back on the bench with a thump. "I—well—I

couldn't pay you all at once, but when summer comes and I work more hours—"

"Colby, be honest," Dr. Voorhees said. "You found Mo on the road. He's a stray."

"He's not! He's mine!"

"You know how I can tell? Because if he'd had someone who cared about him half as much as you do, he wouldn't be half starved and full of burrs and running along one of the most dangerous roads in Kalamazoo County."

I couldn't help it. I broke down all over again, weeping into Van's vest. It had all come to nothing. She wouldn't help, I couldn't afford it, and that car might as well have killed Mo, because now he was going to die by lethal injection or a gun to the head or however they killed animals nobody wanted.

"We already scanned him for an ID chip, but he doesn't have one. I can call the animal shelter and see if anyone's reported a dog like Mo missing. We can put up signs, and I can place an ad online and in the paper. Maybe Mo's owners will turn up. They could pay for the surgery."

I raised my head and glared at her. "You just said he doesn't have an owner! No one who gives a rat's ass about him. No one who'd pay a thousand bucks to save him. Just let me pay for him." My voice cracked. "I don't care whose he was. He's mine now."

We were all silent. The only noises were the dogs barking out back, the horns and revving engines on Harrington Road, and the clock ticking, steady and oblivious, on the wall.

Dr. Voorhees sighed. "I'll tell you what, Colby," she said. "I'll operate on Mo, free of charge."

I stared at her. Van shouted, "That's fantastic!"

Dr. Voorhees held up a hand. "Listen. Colby, you'll still need to pay the other expenses of keeping a dog. Mo will need a full physical exam. He'll need to be tested for worms. He'll need shots for rabies and distemper, repeated annually. You'll need to feed him, of course, and play with him and walk him. You'll need to bring him back to me if he gets sick. You should have him neutered. Keeping a dog is a big responsibility. And strays—well, trust me, they tend to come with baggage. Think about it."

I did. I thought about what Dad might say. I thought about paying for Mo on top of Scarlett. I thought about how I had no idea what to do with him when I was at school and work. Yet nothing seemed as important as getting Mo back on his feet—three of them, anyway.

"Who *doesn't* have baggage?" I said. "Just please take care of Mo."

"It's settled then!" Dr. Voorhees sounded genuinely

happy. "Cindy and I will go ahead and make Mo comfortable for the night."

Van glanced at the clock. "Uh-oh, I have to babysit at six thirty!"

"You'd better get moving then," she said. "I'll call you tomorrow, Colby. If all goes well, Mo should be ready to go home Christmas Eve."

"Can I see him before I go? Just . . . in case?"

Van and I followed Dr. Voorhees back to the green room. Mo was strapped to the steel table. He lay calmly. Without raising his head, he turned his chocolate eyes toward me. I smiled when he flicked his wiry tail. In spite of everything, he didn't hate me. Maybe he even forgave me.

Cindy stepped back from the table. "He's just about cleaned up."

I moved forward and stroked Mo's neck. He kept his eyes on mine.

I made him silent promises. I promised he'd get better. I promised he'd never miss a meal. More than anything, I promised he'd never be alone again.

"I'll see you in two days," I told him, and rushed out before I started blubbering. I hadn't cried so much since Mom died.

"Thank you," I heard Van tell Dr. Voorhees and Cindy.

Outside, snowflakes swirled around us. The winter

wasteland of Harrington Road looked almost beautiful. As we walked to Scarlett, Van asked, "You still want to come over?"

"Yeah, I guess. I've got the eggs." I put my hands in my coat pockets. "Argh!"

"What's wrong?"

I pulled out my left hand, oozing raw, yellow yolk.

Van smirked, and I wiped my hand on his sweatshirt sleeve. Then we laughed so hard my sides ached.

**7**

**VAN MADE US** peanut butter and jelly sandwiches while I bounced Teddy in my arms. Danielle clicked across the linoleum in her high heels, adjusting one large, dangly earring. "Don't keep him up late," she told Van, sticking her head in the fridge. "And no grapes this time, or you're changing his diapers tomorrow." She stuffed a can of Slim-Fast and an issue of *Cosmo* into her purse, kissed Teddy on the top of his head, and slammed the door behind her.

Van and I sat cross-legged on the living room floor, eating our sandwiches while Teddy made a mess of his. Precious stalked by, sniffing at us in a way that said she knew we'd been fraternizing with canines and didn't approve one bit.

"What a day, huh?" Van said.

"Tell me about it. It's like I just woke up from a really weird dream."

"Hey, what's that on your jeans?"

There was a dark-brown smear hardened into the denim. Blood—Mo's blood. Seeing it made me feel strangely good. It was proof that the day *hadn't* been a dream. I could have done without the failed chemistry test, the encounter with Rachel, the hit-and-run accident, and the almost-dead dog, but when all was said and done, I had Mo.

Van brushed the sandwich crumbs from his shirt into his hand, then into the trash. "I'll lend you some sweats. I need to do laundry, anyway. I'll throw your pants and coat—"

"Could you get me some socks, too?" My sockless foot was puckered and freezing.

Van disappeared into his room and returned with a pair of black sweatpants and white tube socks rolled into a tidy ball. I loved borrowing Van's clothes. With their smell of lemon fabric softener, it was like being wrapped up in sunshine and sugar. I changed in the bathroom, rolling up Van's sweats at the ankles.

Back in the living room, Van wiped Teddy's mouth and hands with a dishrag, sniffed his butt, and plunked him back in a pile of blocks and toy cars. I built a little ramp from two triangular blocks and a square. I made a car *vroom* up one side and down the other, while Van told Teddy about our day.

"Then we found a doggy! But the doggy was hurt! So we took him to the doggy doctor!" Teddy stared in googly-eyed wonder, then babbled something incomprehensible. Van nodded wisely. "You're absolutely right. The doctor will make his boo-boos all better."

"Hey," I said, "I just realized we left all those cans out on the road."

Van shrugged. "Whatever. I'll get them tomorrow."

"Unless someone else gets them first."

"Then they probably need the cash as much as I do."

"Have you talked to your mom and Danielle about paying you to babysit?"

"Nope," he said, setting one colored block on top of another.

Danielle worked nights as a cocktail waitress, and Mrs. McIneany worked as a secretary for a travel agency. Van was expected to pick up the slack—like now, while Mrs. McIneany finished Christmas shopping. Van was way better at taking care of Teddy than I was at bagging groceries or cleaning the toilets at Meijer, yet he didn't get paid a thing.

"They're using you."

"Aww, how can you say that when I get to take care

of this cute little guy?" Van leaned into Teddy's neck and blew a raspberry. Teddy squealed and waved his arms in delight. "Some things you do for money. Some things you do for love. Speaking of which, you still haven't come out to your dad, have you?"

I didn't answer.

"I could tell him about me if you want," Van said. "Grease the wheels, you know?"

"No!"

"Why not? It might give him peace of mind knowing I'm not going to impregnate you when he's not around."

"First of all, gross! And second, just no. My dad's a truck driver, Van. A beer-drinking, football-loving, poker-playing, *Playboy*-reading truck driver."

"So?"

Van should have understood better than anyone. His stepmom had freaked when he came out, banning him from their home. He still met up with his dad for bowling or a meal sometimes, but he hadn't seen his stepsisters in years. Fortunately, Van had his mom to fall back on. All I had was Dad—barely.

"Why bother?" I said. "Rachel's over."

"There'll be someone else someday."

"Yeah, maybe when I'm a hundred and five."

Van rolled his eyes. "You're plenty cute, Col. Girls— and I don't just mean Liliana—would be all over you if it wasn't for that cactus impression you do so well. I get itchy just looking at you."

I glowered and stuck out my tongue, which sent Teddy into a fit of giggles.

"Hey, Teddy, want to learn a new word?" I said. "Avalanche!" I pushed my car into Van's tower, twelve teetering blocks high, and the tower tumbled down as Teddy shrieked, "Abbawan! Abbawan!"

My phone rang, and I picked up. "Hey, Dad."

"Bee, how's it going?" I heard talking and clatter in the background—probably a diner.

"I'm fine. I'm hanging out at Van's, watching Teddy."

"Abbawan! Abbawan!"

Dad chuckled. "I can hear that! Good news, Bee. I just stopped for the night outside Memphis. I'll be home Christmas Eve, like we planned."

"Okay," I said, refusing to get too excited. Anything could happen in the next twenty-four hours. "I've put the tree up and everything. And I placed our order for dinner."

"That's great. Thanks for holding down the fort. I'll see you soon."

"Dad?"

"Yes?"

I couldn't think of what to say. I only knew I wanted to hear his voice a little longer. "Nothing. Just, if you see Elvis, say hey for me, okay?"

"You, too," he said. We both laughed, thinking of the old rumor that Elvis was actually alive and working at a Burger King in Kalamazoo. "And say hey to Van and Teddy. Love you, sweetheart."

"Love you, too, Dad. Drive safe." I tucked my phone back in my pocket.

"You didn't tell him," Van said.

"Van, will you lay off? I'll tell him when I'm good and ready. On my own!"

"No, I meant about the dog—about Mo."

"Oh." I bit my lip. "Shit. You're right."

Maybe it was better this way. Why give Dad a chance to argue? No, I'd wait to explain when he was back and there wasn't a thing he could do about it.

Van put Teddy to bed while I took advantage of the McIneanys' not-as-horribly-slow-as-my Internet connection. I waited for Rachel's name to pop up in my inbox. It didn't. No surprise, but I still felt disappointed. Disappointed and stupid.

Van stuck my pants and coat and a bunch of other clothes in the washer, turned on the TV, and popped in *Priscilla, Queen of the Desert,* which we'd seen about fifty times. The bus hadn't made it halfway across Australia before I was drifting off, warm and safe in the crook of Van's arm.

"Did I make the right choice?" I asked sleepily.

"With Mo? How could it be the wrong choice?"

"I don't know. Maybe he'd be better off without me." No maybe about it, in fact. If it weren't for me, he'd still be running along Harrington Road, off to God-knows-where. All I'd wanted was to help him.

"It *was* the right choice," Van said. "And when you pick him up, you'll take one look at him and know for sure."

• • •

My phone woke me at nine the next morning. I rolled off Van's bed to grab it. The number was unfamiliar, but it was local; it wasn't a Tennessee state trooper calling to tell me about an accident. "Hello?"

"Hello, Colby Bingham? This is Dr. Voorhees."

I waited for her to say *Your dog took a turn for the worse last night, sorry. Would you like to scatter the ashes?*

But she didn't. "Everything went fine. No complications. Mo's sleeping off the anesthetic. You've got yourself a three-legged dog!"

A smile crept across my face. "Okay, so—"

"Do you want to pick him up tomorrow? That'll give him some time to recover and you some time to get ready."

"I'm working till four. I can come by after."

"Perfect," said Dr. Voorhees. "See you then."

Van sat up in bed and rubbed the grit from his eyes.

61

"Good news?"

I nodded.

"I promised Danielle I'd take Teddy to see Santa tomorrow. Otherwise I'd go with you."

"It's okay." I took a deep breath. "After everything else, this part will be easy, right?"

8

**From the Rainbow Alliance Internet Lounge:**

**van_the_man:** Vacation, vacation, rockin' the nation . . .

**stonebutterfly:** You're such a cheese ball.

**van_the_man:** Easy there, tiger. I thought this was a "safe space" to express ourselves!

**z-dawg:** What did y'all ask 4 this Chanu-christmakwanzaa?

**rachel_greenbean:** Honestly? To get into Wellesley. I mailed my Early Evaluation app this morning.

**writergrrl:** I was slightly less ambitious. I

asked for a gift certificate to Powell's.

**j0ck25:** I already know what I'm getting: a ticket to the ROSE BOWL!!!!!! Beat that.

**van_the_man:** I asked Santa for a stud muffin to call my own.

**z-dawg:** You better not be macking on Santa. If so, you got some serious daddy issues.

**stonebutterfly:** More like granddaddy issues.

**van_the_man:** Of course not! I told him any of his virile male elves would do. Assuming he's reasonably cute and has a good personality.

**stonebutterfly:** Moving on . . .

**colb33:** Anybody ask for a dog? Because I think it got delivered to the wrong address.

• • •

Winding through the endless aisles at Meijer with my cart, I wondered if this was how new mothers felt the first time they went shopping for their babies. Only, my list was a little different. A large dog collar, into the cart. A six-foot leash. A bag of chow—small for starters, in case Mo's "real" owners turned up. I wondered if Mom felt this way about me, like, *Holy shit, this is actually happening.*

On my way to the clinic I stopped at an ATM and withdrew two hundred dollars from my bank account. It was money for Scarlett's next insurance payment, but I'd just have to scrounge that up later. Back in the vet's lemony waiting room, I stepped up to the counter and cleared my throat. "I'm here to pick up my dog."

*My dog.* Each time I said the words, I believed them more. "His name's Mo."

The receptionist smiled. "Oh, yes, the miracle dog. I saw him tooling around out back. Why don't you have a seat? The vet would like to talk with you before you take Mo home."

I sat on a bench. A middle-aged woman sat at the other end, a cat carrier at her feet. Before long, a man carrying a ball of brown fuzz—either a bite-size dog or an obese guinea pig—emerged from the back with Dr. Voorhees.

"Colby, nice to see you again. Come with me," she said.

I followed her down the hall and out the back door into a yard with a tall, wooden fence. The snowy ground was covered with paw prints. At the far end stood a low building that could have passed for an ordinary garage if it weren't for all the dogs tumbling out through its swinging door, charging toward us. Six of them, all shapes and sizes—and then blunt-nosed, cow-spotted Mo, trotting along behind.

Well, maybe *trotting* wasn't the right word. Mo hobbled like a person on crutches: step, hop, step-step, hop. His right hind leg had vanished, replaced by a wad of white gauze and tape. Around his neck he wore one of those lamp shade collar things.

When he saw me, his tail started wagging, weakly at first, then faster and faster. He made a wobbly beeline for me. I kneeled and opened my arms and was rewarded with muddy paws in my lap and a slobbery tongue in my face.

Dr. Voorhees laughed. "As you can see, he's doing fine. He's still a tad woozy from the anesthetic and had an upset stomach yesterday—the pain meds. But he managed to keep down some breakfast today. Cindy and I took care of his shots and heartworm test. Oh, and gave him a sponge bath. That was first on the agenda! He's a healthy boy."

Mo nudged me with his snout, his lamp shade bonking me. "What's with the, uh—"

"It's called an Elizabethan collar. It'll keep Mo from nibbling at the wound—which, believe me, he'll want to. It's going to be pretty uncomfortable for him for the next few days."

I reached for the wallet in my back pocket. "I brought money."

She waved her hand. "Tina will take care of you before you leave. There's some antibiotic and pain medication waiting for you at the desk, too. I hope you don't mind, but we went ahead and microchipped Mo while he was under."

"Does that mean you don't think his old owners will show up?"

"I can't say," Dr. Voorhees admitted. "But between the chip and his new license, at least if Mo goes wandering again, he'll have ID."

I took the collar and leash from my coat pockets, tore off the price tags, and suited Mo up. Inside, Tina gave me a shiny metal tag to clip onto his collar. "You're official now," I told Mo. "A licensed, professional dog."

Tina gave me Mo's medications, and I counted out enough twenties to cover the bill. There wasn't much to spare. Dr. Voorhees lingered in the hallway. "Why don't you stop by a day or two after Christmas? I want to make sure Mo's leg stays free of infection. It'll be a couple of weeks before the stitches come out."

"Sure thing," I said, and turned to go, Mo trundling

along beside me. I stopped with my hand on the door. "Thanks again, for everything. And, um, Merry Christmas."

"You're welcome," said Dr. Voorhees. "Merry Christmas to you, too."

Out in the lot, I looked down at Mo, and he looked up at me. "Well, Mo. This is it."

Except it wasn't. It had completely slipped my mind that I'd have to get Mo into Scarlett for the drive home. He might be hobbling around fine on three legs, but I didn't think he was up for a flying leap just yet. I opened the passenger door and gnawed my lip. It would have made a great physics problem: how does a shrimpy girl lift a huge, crippled dog into the seat of a Ford pickup? Too bad Van wasn't here to solve it.

Mo stuck his head inside and sniffed the floor enthusiastically. He took a lick at whatever mystery liquid had spilled there. "Mo, stop it! Gross!"

In the end, it took Mo straining with his front legs and scrabbling with his hind leg, and me lifting and pushing his rump, to get him up there. I'm sure anyone driving past had a good laugh at our expense.

At Trail's End I walked Mo through the snow to our front door. *This is my dog at the end of this leash. This is my dog, coming home for the first time.* Before we went in I let Mo clumsily mark the withered juniper bush in front of our trailer.

Mo immediately gave himself the grand tour, hobbling first into my room, then Dad's. He tried to stick his head into the kitchen garbage, but his lamp shade got in the way. Next was the bathroom, and I prayed I'd left the lid down. I also prayed he was housebroken. It dawned on me there was an awful lot I didn't know about Mo.

I fed him and gave him his medicine disguised in a dollop of peanut butter, as Dr. Voorhees had suggested. He licked his bowl until it shone, then looked up at me. You could have played xylophone on his ribs, but I shook my head. "Vet says you might puke it all up."

I sat on the couch with the vet's list of instructions. Mo came over and stood next to me, resting his nose on my thigh. I reached inside the lamp shade to scratch behind his ears, which were crumpled into velvety black triangles. He whined and swished his tail.

"What is it? You just peed. You just ate. I'm petting you. What more could a dog want?"

Mo placed a tentative paw on the couch cushion beside me. It must be confusing for one of your legs to disappear while you're asleep. He looked afraid he'd fall over any second.

"What is it, boy?"

Mo's second paw joined the first, and he craned his great neck until his head was almost higher than mine. He wagged his tail eagerly—so eagerly he nearly knocked the Christmas tree off the coffee table. I slid it away from him.

And when I sat back, I found out exactly what Mo wanted, because suddenly he hopped onto my lap, licking my face.

I went "Oof."

Mo went *Slurp*.

And that's how we spent the rest of the day. It was hours before I realized Dr. Voorhees hadn't returned my star-watching blanket. I guess it hadn't been worth saving.

**M**O AND I WERE snuggled on the couch, watching cheesy Christmas specials on TV, when a key turned in the front door. *Dad!* I hadn't realized until then how much I'd been counting on him making it home for Christmas.

Mo rocketed off the couch with a *woof* that would have scared any intruder. I ran across the room after him, grabbing for his collar and missing. "Shut up, Mo. It's only Dad!"

Dad pushed through the door. Snow dusted his thinning blond hair. He looked tired, as usual. The creases in his forehead deepened as Mo sniffed him from boots to crotch and back down again. "Am I in the right place?"

"Mo, sit," I said helplessly.

"What's going on, Bee?" Dad shut the door but made no move to take off his coat and boots. His pale blue eyes searched mine.

"It's, uh . . ." I dragged Mo away from Dad. His tail thwacked against my shins. "It might not be permanent."

Dad slid off his coat and hung it on the hook by the door, then bent to unlace his boots. He stepped toward us in his socks and held out a hand for Mo to sniff. "When you say it's not permanent—"

"Yes?"

"Do you mean the dog in our living room? Or the fact that he's got only three legs?"

"Ha, ha," I said. "I got him off the clearance rack."

"Please tell me there's a return policy," Dad said with a wry smile.

He rummaged through the fridge for sandwich fixings while I began to tell him the story. Silently, he spread mayonnaise, then mustard, to the edge of the bread and layered on American cheese and salami. He'd eaten the entire thing by the time I finished. Mo sat before him, drooling, the whole time.

Dad dusted his hands over the sink before looking me in the eyes. "Jokes aside, Bee, we've talked about this before. Dogs are a big responsibility. A big expense. They're not toys."

"Dad, did you listen to a word I said? I think I understand Mo's not a box of Tinker Toys left by the side of the road."

"You should've called me before doing anything. We should've discussed it. This is something that affects both of us."

*Please*, I thought. *How does it affect you? You're only here one day a week!* But all I said was "I'm sorry. You're right. But he's here now, and he needs us."

Dad sighed and swiped at his bald spot. "You'll need to pay for—"

"I can handle it."

"You'll need to arrange—"

"I can handle it."

"You'll need to train—"

"I can handle it! Look, Dad, Mo's not going anywhere. He's mine now."

"Unless someone—"

"Right."

"I guess this will be a learning experience," Dad said. "And I do like the idea of you having some protection when you're home alone."

"It'll be fine, Dad. Trust me."

Dad stepped past Mo and hugged me. His flannel

shirt smelled of sweat and French fries and motor oil. "I'll tell you what, Bee: I'm awfully glad to be home," he said. "Dog or no dog."

Mo, sitting beside us, let out a tremendous sigh. *Dog*, he seemed to say. *Definitely dog.*

• • •

Early Christmas morning I woke to the smoky, salty smell of frying bacon. Or I should say, the smell woke Mo, and he woke me by licking my face raw.

Thanks to leaky windows, my room never got truly warm in winter, so I usually slept curled up like a pill bug. Last night, though, I'd thrown off the covers. Mo was a giant, snoring toaster sprawled on the mattress beside me. That wouldn't be a problem until summer, when my room went from icebox to sauna.

New snow had fallen during the night, giving everything soft curves in the glow of Trail's End's security lights. Dad's white rig looked like an igloo at the end of the lot. Mo and I strolled outside, and he attempted to mark every fence post, mailbox, and flowerpot in the park. He had no problem when his target was on the right, since he had his left leg to steady him. But he was still puzzled each time he started to lift his left leg and lost his balance. I couldn't help laughing. "Might as well face it, Mo. You'll never be ambidextrous again."

Dad made eggs, sunny-side up, to go with the bacon. When I was home alone, I skipped out with just a cup of coffee and a slice of toast, but Dad loved to cook breakfast. It was the only meal he liked to cook. He'd even get up extra-early to do it on school days, since his time off didn't fall neatly on the weekends.

We exchanged gifts as we ate. I'd bought Dad a book of travel essays about the American West. Even though he traveled a lot, it wasn't like he had time to hike Yellowstone for a week. I also gave him a good foam pillow for the road; he'd complained that his old one was full of lumps and made his head ache. I hoped he liked it, because I'd already written PROPERTY OF BOB BINGHAM and his phone number on the back with a Sharpie, just in case he left it somewhere by mistake. The pillow didn't look like much, but it was pretty expensive.

Dad gave me a mall gift card, some fruity-smelling bath products, and a new soccer ball. "For my favorite jock," he said. "Maybe this year you can get back on the team, huh?"

I leaned around the table to give him a sidearm hug. "Thanks, Dad."

I didn't have the heart to tell him I had no plans to return to my soccer career.

"There's a box of stuff for Scarlett outside," Dad said. He turned to Mo. "Sorry, fella. If I'd known you'd

be here, maybe I'd have brought you something, too."
He flipped Mo a strip of bacon. It bounced off his nose,
then disappeared down his throat with a whole lot of lip
smacking.

Grammy and Pop-Pop called from Florida, which
was pleasantly pointless as always, and then Aunt Sue,
who was visiting them, took her turn. It was funny
watching Dad talk on the phone with her. His face
looked as if he were being spooned cough medicine as he
said things like "Didn't I *say* I'd make it home in time?"
and "Well, the Weather Channel was wrong. The roads
were fine," and "Sue, I've been driving professionally
for twenty years! I know how to handle snow."

It was funny until he shoved the phone into my
hands.

"Hi, Aunt Sue," I mumbled. "How's Florida?"

"You have no idea how sunny and warm it is! Do you
know what I'm wearing right now?"

"Um . . . what?"

"A sundress, sandals, and forty-five sunblock. Sheer
heaven. It's a wonder I've stayed in Michigan all these
years. But then, you and your father would have nobody,
wouldn't you?"

"Not exactly," I said. "We've got a dog now."

"Oh. Is that so." I wasn't sure if Aunt Sue sounded
pissed because she hadn't been consulted or because I'd

suggested a dog was an adequate replacement for her. "That's an interesting development. What possessed your father? You realize I can't have a dog in my house. It's against condo regulations, not to mention it would damage my floors."

As if I planned to stay at her place ever again. "I know," I said. "Don't worry. You won't have to do a thing."

"Well, I should hope not. But are you sure your father knows what he's doing? He's never owned a pet in his life. Did you know he never even changed a diaper until you came along? Put him on the line again."

I started to give Dad the phone, but he dodged away, looking panicked. "He's in the bathroom," I lied. "Do you want me to have him call you back later?"

"If you would," Aunt Sue said. "But tell him not to bother past noon. We're having dinner with the neighbors. They have their own pool! I can't wait to try out my new bathing suit. It's one of those cute little— what's the word?—tankinis."

I hung up, trying very hard not to imagine pasty Aunt Sue in a swimsuit, much less a two-piece. I bet the tankini was much cuter without her inside of it.

"What else did she want to bust my chops about?" Dad asked.

"You and Aunt Sue have something in common," I

said. "You both think owning a dog is a bad idea. She wants to convince you that you're either incompetent or insane."

Dad flushed and pressed his lips together. "That's it, Bee," he said. "Mo's staying."

I turned away to hide my grin.

After an afternoon of football—first on TV, then out in the snow—Dad and I shoveled out Mom's old Chevy, and he drove into town to pick up our Christmas dinner at Meijer.

The three of us feasted.

That night as Mo and I made our final rounds of Trail's End, I stopped and looked up at the sky. The wind had shoved the clouds to the horizon. The stars were tiny silver boats floating on a sea of black. I thought of Rachel, the warmth of her shoulder against mine as we lay side by side in the back of my truck staring up at the stars—not kissing or talking, just absorbing it all.

Then Mo tugged on his leash, and I came back to reality. It was just me and my dog now.

**10**

THE THING ABOUT living in a trailer park is that you can't bring home, say, a three-legged dog without attracting attention. It wasn't just ancient, possibly senile Mr. Harmon on the one side of us or the Van Der Beeks on the other who ventured out to admire Mo and give him a pat on the head (which he always responded to with a giant production of tail wagging and sloppy kisses). Neighbors who'd never squinted at me twice came out on their stoops when Mo and I paraded by, to ask questions and give commentary: how to walk him, what to feed him, blah, blah, blah.

Mo had no fans more devoted than the Van Der Beek kids. Morning, evening, it didn't matter; we couldn't step out the door without the four of them ambushing us. "It's like they do nothing all day but wait to attack," I told Van over the phone. "They yell 'Geronimo' when they see him. They think it's the most hilarious thing ever."

Van giggled. "Geroni-mo. That's pretty good . . . if you ignore the fact that Geronimo was a Native American military leader, and Mo's main talent is butt sniffing."

When I took Mo back to the clinic, Dr. Voorhees checked his wound for infection, and Cindy changed his dressing. "Not a peep from Animal Control," Dr. Voorhees said. "And I haven't heard back on the ad yet, either. Did you see it? I posted it on Craigslist and in the *Gazette*."

She retrieved a newspaper from the reception desk, flipped to the classified section, and pointed. I read: "FOUND DOG: Male b&w bulldog mix, 70 lb. Found on Harrington Rd, 12/22." A dull ache began in my gut as I remembered how temporary this whole situation might be. Mo's real owners could show up next week or tomorrow or five minutes from now, and he'd return to whatever lousy life he'd led before he hit the road and the road hit back.

Dr. Voorhees looked sympathetic. "Never mind that now. Mo's safe and getting better, and that's what's most important." She wrote instructions on her pad for reducing his pain meds, tore off the slip, and put it in my hand. "Call me if he has any problems."

He didn't. But as winter break rolled on, I wished I hadn't put in for so many shifts. When I came home from work one afternoon, Mo rushed to the door as usual, his tail a blur. I guess he hoped I'd be so thrilled, too, that I wouldn't notice the coffee grounds and gnawed burger wrappers and banana peels strewn across the floor.

"Damn dog!" I yelled as I grabbed the broom, but I stopped when Mo dodged away from me, cringing. Which was worse: a mess on the floor or a dog who was terrified I'd beat him with the broomstick? "Damn dog," I repeated softly as I swept up the garbage.

Mo crept forward and licked my hand in apology.

I could only blame myself for not stashing the garbage can in the bathroom. I'd learned to shut the bathroom door after finding the furniture mummified with shredded toilet paper. I'd learned to shut the bedroom doors after finding my old soccer cleats on the couch, covered with teeth marks. It was tempting to let Mo have them, but I didn't trust him to know the difference between shoes that had outlived their purpose and those I actually cared about. Meanwhile, he kept scraping his stump along the floor to scratch it. I'd had to retape his gauze a million times.

Winter break was half over, and Rachel hadn't called

yet. When my phone woke me late on the morning of New Year's Eve, I dived for it. I couldn't think of a better way for us to start over than with a kiss at midnight.

But it was Van. "Quick," he said, "Danielle has this idea I'm babysitting tonight, but I told her I already have plans."

"Good for you!"

"Yeah, except I don't. Can we make some, fast? There's that all-ages party the Gay and Lesbian Resource Center has—the one we went to last year. That was fun."

"No way. Only losers without a real party go to that party," I said, even though Van was right; last year it had been really fun. Last year when I'd been so eager to meet girls, to dance and flirt and maybe have something come of it. Nothing had happened that night, but I'd felt absolutely free to be myself, unjudged and unafraid in a way I never felt at school.

Van said nothing.

"Please don't make me go," I said. "New Year's Eve is all about couples."

Van said nothing.

"I'm over Rachel, okay? I'm just not ready for someone else."

"Well, maybe *I'm* ready," Van said.

Immediately, I felt ashamed. Last year at midnight

Van and I had stood at the side of the dance floor and hugged before clinking glasses of sparkling white grape juice with everyone else. After a whole year of being single, of course he was hoping for more. I took a deep breath and dug my fingers into Mo's ruff. He squirmed onto his back so I could massage his belly. "I'm sorry," I said. "You're right. Let's go."

• • •

That night I left Mo with his new batch of chew toys and revved up Scarlett. It was bitterly cold, and her engine choked a few times before roaring to life. I'd put on my nicest jeans and my dressiest shirt: a pink, sparkly pullover. I even put on lip gloss and stuck the tube in my coat pocket for later. There was no point in looking like a slob, even if I was only going for Van's sake.

At the McIneanys', Van hopped in, his breath clouding around his head. He bounced up and down in his seat. The springs squeaked.

"Excited much?" I asked, pulling onto Harrington Road.

Van looked away. "Just cold."

Something sweet tingled in my nostrils. "Is that cologne I smell?"

Van sank so low the shoulders of his down vest came up to his ears.

We headed downtown, where I managed, after

about fifty tries, to parallel park Scarlett a couple of blocks from the party. The GLRC had rented out a nearby church for the event. We ran all the way there, our sneakers skidding on the slick sidewalks. We were greeted by a blast of warm air and remixed eighties music pumping through the sound system. Most of the crowd were middle-aged, button-down adults who probably volunteered at the center, but there were a fair number of teenagers who, like us, didn't have somewhere else to be. There were a couple of other kids from the Alliance, but no one I usually hung out with. Rachel, of course, was nowhere in sight.

Van started flailing to the music. I shimmied beside him, hands in the air. And everything was fine until a guy with a jagged, black mohawk whisked Van away.

Suddenly, I was aware of a girl standing solo across the room trying to catch my eye. When I looked away, there was a different girl alone in a different corner. I didn't want to dance with them, bump shoulders with them, feel them soft and vulnerable through their shirts, hoping the negative space in our hearts would somehow add up to a positive. What I wanted was for Rachel to walk in and tell me Michael was history.

I retreated to the snack table, ladled myself a cup of sticky-sweet punch, and shoved a handful of sugar cookies into my mouth. A slow song came on, and Van spun by with Mohawk Boy, cheek pressed against the taller boy's shoulder. He winked at me, and I gave him a halfhearted thumbs-up. I hoped their romance lasted until midnight, at least. One of us deserved a kiss.

I didn't realize the butch girl in the leather jacket had her eyes on me, and not the tray of cookies beside me, until she asked if I wanted to dance. Her face was friendly, but I hesitated. "You don't have to think so hard," she said. "It ain't like I asked you to prom."

"I can't," I managed. "I'm sorry. It's not you, believe me. I just—I can't."

The girl's lips pinched together, and she walked away. A couple of minutes later I saw her dancing with some other girl. I edged away from the snacks, hoping I could melt into the shadows and stay there until the countdown and kisses were over.

No such luck. Fifteen minutes later, after turning down the third girl who'd asked me to dance, I dodged my way across the room and tapped Van on the shoulder. "Can I cut in?"

Mohawk Boy sneered at me, but Van squeezed his arm. "Back in a sec." He put his hands on my waist and started bouncing again.

"I've got to go," I hollered above the pulsing beat.

"What? You're kidding! We practically just got here!"

"I was hoping you could get a ride back with someone else." I nodded at Mohawk Boy.

"Ohhh." A smile appeared on Van's face. "I think that can be arranged!" Then he frowned. "Are you okay?"

"I'm fine! It's just—" I couldn't tell him the truth, not without another lecture on the vast number of fish in the sea. "I'm worried about Mo."

Van was too giddy to argue. "Okay! Drive safe! Happy New Year!" He whirled off.

I wanted to go straight to bed. But when I pulled into Trail's End, it was seething with kids and dads setting off firecrackers. Not the small, fizzling kind, either. You could tell from the bangs and showers of sparks that they'd been bought from warehouses across the Indiana border. The Van Der Beeks hooted at me, their faces devilish in the glare. I wouldn't be sleeping any time soon.

When I pushed open the front door, Mo didn't scamper to greet me. I'd left a light on for him, so I quickly saw the big, yellow puddle on the kitchen linoleum. Mo's first accident. "Mo!" I called over the crackle and boom of the firecrackers outside. No answer.

"Mo?" I crept across the living room. Maybe some

psycho had broken in and killed Mo and was now hiding in the bathroom or my bedroom closet waiting to cut my throat. A cold sweat broke out on my forehead.

I barely breathed as I pushed open my bedroom door. Nothing there. Nothing in my dad's room or the bathroom. Of course—I'd left all the doors shut, so unless Mo had sprouted opposable thumbs while I was out—

I called again, voice breaking, "Mo! Where are you?"

A rustle came from the direction of the couch, and the curtains behind it stirred. At last Mo toddled from behind the couch, his tail tucked tightly under him, his lamp shade collar knocked askew.

"You poor thing! The noise must've terrified you." I threw my arms around him and squeezed him to me before taking off my coat and cleaning up the mess. He watched warily from a distance. "I'm not going to hit you, for God's sake. Just don't make a habit of it, okay?" He made a noise: part sigh, part whimper. I took it as "Okay."

There was no point walking Mo now. He flinched every time a firecracker went off, and his bladder was already empty. I removed his lamp shade, sat on the couch, and tuned the TV to Times Square, my phone nearby in case Dad or Van decided to call. Mo meekly climbed up beside me and settled down with his head in my lap. I pulled a blanket off the back of the couch and draped it over us.

"Happy New Year," I said, stroking Mo's floppy black ears.

Mo's only answer was a low, doggy snore.

11

**THE NEXT MORNING** I went to work raccoon-eyed. Eight hours of bagging frozen pizzas and canned tuna, not to mention mopping up unspeakable messes in the public restrooms, did nothing to improve my mood. When I got home, I barely had the energy to take Mo out for a pit stop. I was grateful the Van Der Beeks were too busy playing Blow Up the Kitchen, Tie Up the Baby, or whatever it was they did when they weren't playing Ninjas, to jump us.

Maybe I shouldn't have answered the phone when I saw it was Rachel, but I couldn't stop myself. I slowly pressed my thumb to the remote, silencing the TV. "Hey."

"Hey," she said. "I just called to say hi. And Happy New Year."

"Hi and Happy New Year yourself." I plopped back against the couch cushions, and Mo flopped against me.

"How's your break going? Did you do anything fun last night?"

I longed to tell Rachel I'd spent the whole night in the arms of some amazing, gorgeous girl. But what if she was happy for me, relieved she hadn't permanently broken my heart?

I decided on half the truth. "Not much. Watched the ball drop in Times Square. You?"

"I went to this party at the JCC with Michael. And his parents and my parents."

"JCC?"

"Jewish Community Center."

"Oh."

"It was pretty dorky. Lots of dumb games and hokey music." Rachel laughed a little. "You weren't alone, were you? You were with Van?"

"Actually, I hung out with Mo." I smiled, imagining her confusion. *Who's Mo? Is Mo short for Maureen?* I added casually, "Mo's my dog."

"Oh, um, I saw what you wrote in the Lounge, but I thought you were kidding. I thought your dad—"

"He changed his mind."

"How did— Where did—"

"It's kind of a long story."

"I've got time."

"Do you really? Because I'd hate to interfere with your college applications or your plans with Michael."

Rachel sighed. I pictured her shuffling her feet, fidgeting with the phone. "I called to ask if you wanted to hang out before school starts. There's only a few days left."

My heart leapt. "What do you want to do?"

"I don't know. Watch a movie? Play cards? And you could tell me all about Mo."

My organs sank back to their usual places. Well, what had I expected her to say? *Drive to the lake, lie under the stars, and kiss until our lips bruise?* Cards, a movie—they were nothing, like I was a sniveling kid at the checkout counter whose mom buys a bag of Skittles just to make it shut up.

I remembered a time at the park last fall. Van had been off skateboarding or something; it was just the two of us. Rachel and I had dribbled my soccer ball down to the creek bank and then pulled off our shoes and socks, rolled up our pant legs to our knees, and gone wading, her hand in mine. The water had been so cold I had to bite my tongue to keep from yelling, and the pebbles at the bottom hadn't felt nearly as smooth as they'd looked.

Rachel had gotten this thoughtful expression on her

face and said, "Wow. This water is really, really cold. And these rocks are really, really sharp." Then she grinned at me. "But it's totally worth it, isn't it?"

It had been: standing shin deep in icy creek water, freezing my ass off while the girl I loved smiled at me, only me.

What changed for her? Why hadn't I been worth it?

On the phone, Rachel was still waiting. But what could I possibly say that would make things right between us? I stroked Mo's neck.

"Should I even bother?" she said.

"Bother what?"

"Anything. Talking to you. Trying to be friends."

So I could still get through to her—make her feel something, even if it was only anger. "Maybe you shouldn't bother," I said. "Maybe I'm not worth it."

"You know that isn't what I meant. But look, Colby, you don't make this easy."

"Is that my job? You're the one who broke up with me, Rachel."

"I know! Trust me, I feel plenty guilty already."

"Then why'd you do it?" I hated the whiny note in my voice.

"I tried to explain," Rachel said. "That last night, I tried."

"What are you talking about?"

Rachel sighed again, a huff of static. "Things with Michael aren't easier just because he's a guy. It's who he is. He likes school. He's got all these plans for college and his career. I never have to worry about him."

"You didn't *have* to worry about me."

"Yes, I did!" Her ferocity startled me. "You think I didn't care about you, but you're wrong. How do you think it made me feel, knowing you didn't give a shit about anything?"

"I gave a shit about you! I gave a whole lot more than a shit."

"I know that, but what else? Everything is fine with you, everything is fun, it doesn't matter if you're flunking out, it doesn't matter if you bag groceries for the rest of your life. I can't stand that you talk like these things don't matter. They *do* matter. They matter a lot."

"Well, sorry I'm not perfect, but things haven't exactly been easy since—"

"Since your mom died. I know. But, Colby, it's been almost two years."

If Rachel had been in the room with me, I don't know what I would have done. Slapped her? Run away? Blood rushed to my head, and my hands felt icy. "If your mother were dead," I said, "you'd know it's not that simple. But she's not, so shut up, okay?"

"Okay, but tell me this," Rachel said. "What do you

think your mom would say if she knew you were failing out? Do you think she'd be proud?"

"Don't you dare put words in her mouth," I said. "You never even knew her!"

"You're right," she said quietly. "And I never will, because you know what? You never talk about her. Just like you never talk about anything serious. 'Pretend it doesn't exist,' isn't that what you say?"

I fumed silently.

"Look, Colby, isn't it enough that I just don't think we're right for each other? It's not like we would've stayed together forever. Next year I'll be going away to college, and you'll—"

She didn't need to finish, and I didn't let her. I threw the phone on the floor.

• • •

The phone rang again after Mo and I had gone to bed. I hoped it was Dad. I knew he'd be home the next day, but maybe he was calling to wish me a Happy New Year.

I should have known it would be Van. "Ask me if I'm a boat."

"Uh, okay, freak. Are you a boat?" I said.

"Yes. Ask me if I'm a truck."

"Are you a truck?"

"No, silly monkey, I just told you I was a boat!"

"I'm hanging up."

"Well. Crappy New Year to you, too."

"I had another fight with Rachel."

"Oh. Wow. Want to talk about it?"

"Honestly? No. How did things go for you last night? You know, nudge-nudge, wink-wink."

"Oh, that. It went fine till we got to his place, and he got out a bowl and a dime bag."

"What'd you tell him?"

"That I wasn't going to dull my senses with drugs or alcohol, and I hoped he felt the same way."

"And?"

"He laughed at me and asked where I've been, straight edge is so last week. Like it's something I do to be cool!"

It didn't seem like the right time to remind Van that it wasn't particularly straight edge to hop into bed with a boy you'd just met at a party. "Screw him," I said. "He's a loser."

"He was so hot, though. Did you see his eyelashes? They were amazing! Like beautiful black spiders."

"What'd you do next?"

"Called a cab. As if I wasn't broke already." There was a long pause as each of us reflected on the utter lousiness of the past twenty-four hours. Finally, Van said, "I've made a resolution."

"Oh, yeah? You haven't resolved for me to make

honor roll again, have you?"

"I'm afraid I've given up on that. No, this one's better."

"You're going to demand fair payment for babysitting Teddy?"

"You've got to think bigger. Listen closely, Col, because this is the year our lives are truly going to change for the better."

"You've found a way to rig the lottery. You've invented a time machine. We're moving to Tahiti and selling our bodies to rich American tourists."

"Don't be ridonkulous. And why does your mind always go right to money?"

*Because if I were rich, Dad could quit his job and come home.*

Van plunged on. "This is the year that you, Colby Bingham, and I, Donovan McIneany, find true love. No more girls waiting for boyfriends. No more unbelievably sexy punks who think straight edge is nothing more than the flavor of the week. We're going to set our sights on people who deserve us as much as we deserve them. Then aim, lock, fire Cupid's missile of love!"

"And you call me ridonkulous," I said.

**STUMBLED OUT** of my room the next morning to find Dad frying up sausage links and omelets. "Happy Happy, Bee!" he called from the stove. "Happy Happy" is, for some reason, what truck drivers say instead of "Happy New Year." They also say "Merry Merry" instead of "Merry Christmas," so go figure.

"Happy Happy to you, too," I said, hugging him.

Dad ruffled my hair. He smelled like strawberries and mint. He must have been so tired from driving half the night that he grabbed my new, fruity body wash instead of his own. "How are you?" he asked, releasing me.

"Not terrible." I dumped a couple of scoops of chow into Mo's bowl. Mo took his eyes off the sausages long enough to snarf that up, then went back to drooling at the stove. I set the table and poured our orange juice. Behind me, I heard a sausage link being gulped in midair by a dog with a bottomless stomach. I smiled and shook my head.

"You catch the Bowl games yesterday?" Dad asked as we sat down to eat.

"Nah, I had work. Did you?"

"Tuned in to a couple. Whenever the FM cut out, someone filled me in on the CB. Nothing like watching it on TV, but you make do." Dad popped another bite of omelet into his mouth. "How was your New Year's?"

I rolled my sausage links from one side of the plate to the other, then back. "Boring. How about yours?"

"Fine, fine. I met up with some folks outside Denver for a bit." He trailed off. "You remember John Gruber? Hauls timber?"

"I guess so." Dad had lots of friends on the road, more than he did at home. How could he expect me to keep them straight when I'd never even met them? "What about him?"

"He's landed a short-haul job down in Athens, Georgia. I probably won't see him again."

I stabbed a sausage link with my fork and bit off the end.

"But that's how it is out there. You make a friend

just to lose a friend. You don't dare get used to anything; before long it'll change."

I guess he wanted me to admire this profound observation, to mourn the loss of one of his faceless trucker buddies. But all I could think was *Yay for John Gruber. Yay for John Gruber's family, having Daddy home for good.* I'd had such a small taste of that, and the circumstances had been rotten.

"Dad? Do you ever think about doing that? Taking a short-haul job, I mean."

"Bee, you know those jobs are hard to come by. The pay's not as good, either. We're still paying off your mom's medical bills, and I want you to have money for college."

I thought of my failed chemistry test and my other steadily declining grades but kept my mouth shut. If he wanted his little college fantasy, he could have it. It was less trouble that way, for both of us.

"I know our arrangement isn't ideal, but the work's reliable. It keeps us living comfortably." Dad pushed back his chair and carried his empty plate to the sink.

The conversation was over.

I grabbed Mo's leash and took him out into the bitter cold morning, thinking about those short months Dad had been home: Mom's final weeks and the weeks that followed. It had been so strange. First, the shock, even though we'd known the end was coming; we couldn't get used to it, couldn't accept it. Dad and I had stumbled around with red eyes and didn't care who noticed. The phone had rung constantly. Grammy and Pop-Pop had swooped in from Florida and fluttered around us like anxious birds. We'd eaten Aunt Sue's overbaked casseroles for two weeks straight. At night I'd fall asleep on the couch, my head in Dad's lap as he watched TV shows about the pyramids and Machu Picchu and the Great Barrier Reef. When he was tired, he'd lie on the floor beside me and sleep, not bothering to turn off the lights or the TV.

Then, suddenly, there had been silence. The phone calls and visits stopped. Dad had sent me back to school, and he had gone back to work. Life was normal again—sort of.

Dad's evenings and weekends away had never seemed so long until I had to face them on my own. Even when we were together, things weren't the same. We didn't know what to say to each other, what to do. We hadn't realized our lives revolved around Mom.

*This is what you call comfortable, Dad? Sleeping behind the driver's seat? Driving through nights and weekends and holidays when you ought to be here with me?*

The day Mom's diagnosis had gotten pushed from

Stage III to Stage IV, she'd called Dad. He bobtailed home from Virginia, even though driving without a load meant losing money.

Mom and I had sat on the couch, waiting for him. I was only five feet tall and a hundred and ten pounds, but I felt like a giant compared to Mom. Over the past few months, she'd turned into a doll made of toothpicks and tissue paper.

"It's going to get harder now, Bee," she'd said.

I didn't respond.

"You've been so strong in all this. A real trouper."

I still didn't respond. I didn't even nod.

"I know Aunt Sue isn't your favorite person." I'd been staying with Sue while Mom was at the hospital and Dad was away. "Hell, even with all she's done for us, she's not my favorite person, either. But since all this began, I haven't heard you complain."

I'd looked down at my hands and picked at a cuticle. My nails were a ragged mess.

"I want you to stay strong, okay? Stronger than ever." Mom shook my knee. "Bee?"

Shutting my eyes, I croaked, "I'll try."

"Good," Mom had said, pulling me tight against her bony chest, "because Daddy's going to need your help. When—if something happens to me, you'll be all he's got."

It turned out to be even harder than I thought. Still, I tried. I never whined about the long days alone. I never begged Dad to come home.

But that didn't mean I wasn't waiting for him to do it on his own. He'd laid out the arguments for OTR trucking as neatly as Mom's clothes before we took them to Goodwill, but something never quite fit. If I was all he had, why wasn't I more important than medical bills or a college fund? The only explanation I could come up with was that he had a new girlfriend out there but didn't have the guts to admit it. That, or he just didn't want to be with me.

**13**

**MO WAGGED HIS TAIL** wildly as I herded him into Scarlett on Friday morning. "If you knew what was coming," I said, "you wouldn't be so happy." Soon we were back at the clinic, shut into an examining room with Cindy. Mo shivered on the steel table, tail tucked beneath him. I stroked his head and neck, but his eyes accused me: *We could be at home on the couch right now if it weren't for you.*

Cindy looked Mo over and asked questions about his energy and appetite, both good. Then Dr. Voorhees came in. "Today's the day!" she told Mo, slipping him a biscuit. He sniffed it suspiciously before biting down. "We'll get rid of those nasty stitches in a jiffy."

Dr. Voorhees stripped the gauze from Mo's stump.

His eyes grew wide when she plucked with scissors and tweezers at the black thread lacing his wound. His nails skidded on the table as he tried to wriggle away. Cindy held him so firmly I wondered if she'd been one of those girls in high school who joined the wrestling team. When the stitches were gone, Dr. Voorhees unsnapped Mo's lamp shade and set it on the counter.

Mo was left with a long, pink, puckered scar and lots of stubble where his fur was just starting to grow back. Cindy lowered him to the floor, and he slunk behind my legs. I leaned down to stroke his ears. "Dr. Voorhees, there still hasn't been any—"

"News? No. It's been what, two weeks? Colby, I think it's time to stop thinking of Mo as temporary and accept that you're in this for the long haul."

I hugged Mo, and he gave me the most slobbery kiss in the universe. I'd never been so glad to be in anything for the long haul.

"How are you adjusting to being a pet owner?" Dr. Voorhees asked.

"Well, I'm beginning to understand what everyone says about a dog being a big responsibility," I admitted. "He keeps finding new things to get into. And he's impossible to walk! One minute he's running his nose over every inch of ground. Then he's yanking me off my feet to chase some invisible squirrel."

She laughed. "Can you come back at five fifteen? With Mo, of course. I'll give you some tips on handling him."

"Oh no. You don't have to do that."

"Don't be silly. It's no trouble at all. I wish more people took an interest in their pets' behavior. It would save me a lot of trouble. Besides, I know Mo sort of dropped from the sky on you."

*Like the klutziest angel ever.*

"Well, if you're sure," I said.

• • •

When we returned, there was only one car in the lot: a green SUV with Dog Is My Copilot and ASPCA bumper stickers. It had to be Dr. Voorhees's. Mo was not exactly thrilled to be back. I had to drag him into the empty waiting room. I gave a nervous cough to announce our presence as Mo hunched behind my legs.

Dr. Voorhees came in. "Oh good, you made it. Colby, take off your coat, and we'll get started."

I draped my coat over a bench, then turned to Mo. Since we hadn't hauled him into an examining room or poked at his stump, he was starting to relax. It didn't hurt when Dr. Voorhees pulled a dog biscuit from her pocket and held it out to him.

Dr. Voorhees showed me how to fix his collar and leash high on his neck, just behind his ears, to give me more control. She strode out of the waiting room and down the hall, Mo hobbling meekly at her heel as if he weren't the same dog who'd yanked me off my feet and into a snowdrift that very morning. When they reached the end of the hall, she turned, and he toddled on back.

Then it was my turn. We passed the bathroom, various examining rooms, and finally the operating room. Every now and then Dr. Voorhees called to me to keep my arm relaxed or showed me how to correct Mo and bring his attention back to me. And, amazingly, instead of Mo dragging me or vice versa, we walked side by side.

"It won't be this easy every time," Dr. Voorhees warned me, "especially with all the distractions of the outdoors. But you'll get it. Give Mo a nice, long walk to tire him out before you leave in the morning—or a jog, if you both can manage it—and hopefully he won't have the extra energy to spend tearing the house apart."

I pulled on my coat. Dr. Voorhees said, "If you'd like to come back next Friday, we can work on 'sit' and 'stay.'"

"Dr. Voorhees—"

"Please, call me Robyn."

"Uh, Robyn. I appreciate what you're doing. I mean, thanks. But you've already done so much for Mo and me. I can't ask for more."

A look I couldn't pin down flashed across her face. Then she smiled. "I meant what I said, Colby: it's no trouble. Mo's such a sweet boy. It's a pleasure to work with him."

She walked to the door and opened it for us. Cold air swirled in around our feet. "Be patient with her, Mo," Dr. Voorhees—Robyn—said, patting his head. "Colby has a lot to learn."

• • •

School began again, with only two weeks left in the semester. I dutifully went to all my classes, not because I minded detention—I did some of my best daydreaming in detention—but because I needed to go home to Mo as soon as the bell rang. Unfortunately, sitting through school confirmed what I'd suspected: I'd fallen so far behind over the fall, there was no way I could catch up before finals. This report card would not be pretty.

When activity period rolled around on Wednesday afternoon, I debated whether to head to Mr. Peabody's room for the Alliance meeting. I dreaded seeing Rachel. On the other hand, why should I be the one to give it up, especially now that she had a boyfriend?

Mr. Peabody greeted me outside the door. "*Colby* Bingham! It's great to have you back. How was your vacation?"

"Okay, I guess. I got a dog."

"Okay? You *guess*? Getting a dog sounds way more than okay to me!" Mr. Peabody gripped my shoulders and gave me a little shake. A smile slipped onto my face, and he beamed. "That's more like it! You'll have to tell me all about it sometime."

"What about you?" I asked. "Did you have a good break?"

"Yes, indeedy. Andrew and I took Lucy to Disney World. We went on the teacups, and I'll tell you what: I never knew such a little girl could have so much puke in her!" He looked proud. "Come on. Let's go see if we've got a quorum."

When we walked into the classroom, I was amazed by how many people smiled at me, even some newer members I didn't really know. Liliana waved and pointed to the empty chair between her and Zak. Then I saw him. Sitting beside Rachel in the circle, chatting up his neighbors as if he had every right to be there, was Michael Schmidt.

I backed out of the room and sagged against a locker. I shut my eyes. Did he think a single trip to Fazoli's made him one of us?

Rapid footsteps approached. "Colby." It was Rachel. "I didn't think you'd come."

"Why's he here, Rachel?"

"It's a gay-straight alliance." Her tone was defensive.

"He's a straight ally."

"And here I thought he'd come out of the closet over break."

"Look, I'm sorry. But it's been so long since you've been to a meeting, I thought you'd quit."

"Well, I'm sorry to disappoint you. But don't worry, I'm leaving now." I took a step away.

Rachel reached out and touched my sleeve. "Don't be like this. No Name-Calling Week is coming up. We need you."

"No, you don't, actually. You've got enough members already. More than enough." Another step.

"Do you want me to ask him to leave?" There was a growing edge to Rachel's voice. "I can do that."

"I don't want you to do anything. But if he cares so much, where was he before you two hooked up? Changing lives through chess club?"

"He didn't know much about it," Rachel said. "When I told him how we try to make school a more accepting place for everyone, he wanted to see what it was like for himself. He's really not a bad person, Colby. He's actually a pretty great guy."

"Obviously. You'd never settle for anything less."

Then I walked away for real. Rachel didn't try to stop me.

***From the Rainbow Alliance Internet Lounge:***

**van_the_man:** ZOMG, so psyched for the AVD!!!

**colb33:** The what?

**yinyang:** Alternative Valentine's Dance. You know the Valentine's Dance that the student council puts on every year? We're going to do our own queer dance.

**kittykat96:** I for one do not completely agree with this plan. How can we expect the rest of the school to treat us the same as everybody else if we keep ourselves separate?

**van_the_man:** I'd like to dance with a boy and not worry about getting bashed.

**writergrrl:** I'd like to dance with girls and not worry about it getting back to my parents. Not to mention I can't even dance with boys without feeling guilty about the double standard.

**rachel_greenbean:** Besides, the dances are on different nights. You can go to both if you want.

**colb33:** I know I wasn't at the meeting, but . . . I'm having a hard time imagining

110

an Alliance dance. Are we going to have it in Mr. P.'s room and play tunes off his computer? Turn the light switch on and off and pretend we're at a rave?

**yinyang:** No need to be snarky. We're going to reserve the cafeteria and invite kids from all the other high schools in Kalamazoo County.

**van_the_man:** WOO HOO PARTY!!!

**writergrrl:** I'll ask if I can write up an article for The Watchman. Maybe we can recruit more members for the Alliance while we're at it.

**schmitty:** Great idea! You've already got my approval as features editor.

• • •

As if he hadn't done enough to ruin my life, Michael Schmidt had infiltrated the Lounge.

**14**

**I**'D BEEN ALL SET to let Robyn's offer of training slide by. She'd probably forgotten, anyway. But she called me Friday after school. "You and Mo up for another lesson tonight?"

"Uh, sure. I mean, I don't have any plans."

"Come up to the house this time—second floor, above the clinic. Some people feel like they live at their jobs, but I literally do." She laughed. "There's a set of stairs outside, around back. Just come up and knock."

I hesitated. It was bad enough intruding on her personal time. I didn't want to invade her home, too.

She misinterpreted my silence. "If Mo's not up to stairs, I'll come down. But we'd be more comfortable up there."

"All right," I said. "See you at five fifteen."

• • •

I helped Mo scrabble up the wooden stairs to Robyn's place. The door at the top swung open before I could knock. "Come in, come in, Colby and Mo."

She'd exchanged her white coat and pants for a Detroit Lions sweat suit. Crowding around her knees was a posse of dogs. I counted three snuffling noses, not including Mo's. "Back off," Robyn told them cheerfully, and ushered us out of the cold and into the not-much-warmer house. My breath puffed around me.

"I leave the heat off during the day since the dogs are out back," she explained, taking my coat and hanging it on the rack by the door. "It'll warm up soon. I thought we'd have a cup of tea in the meantime."

I edged into the kitchen, with its homey red and gold decor, the strangeness of the situation sinking in. Seeing Robyn in a sweat suit was weird enough; it couldn't have been much worse if she'd worn a flannel nightie. Traipsing through her house was even more awkward, like going to a teacher's house. Maybe she was comfortable up here, but right then I would have preferred the antiseptic feel of the clinic.

She filled the kettle at the tap, oblivious.

I unclipped Mo's leash, and he quickly stuck his nose under the tails of the other three dogs. They returned the greeting. I perched on a stool by the kitchen island

and watched. "Are these your only dogs?"

"Only?" Robyn exclaimed. "Three isn't enough for you?"

"There were at least six here the day I picked up Mo."

"Ah. The rest were Christmas boarders who've gone home. This is Oscar"—she pointed her toe at a cinnamon-colored fuzz ball now snuffling for crumbs along the linoleum—"and that shepherd mix sniffing your coat is Lorraine. And that curly, gray butt slinking away is Fontine, my toy poodle. Don't be offended. She's a snob around strangers."

Robyn opened a cupboard and took down a glass cookie jar filled with dog biscuits. She offered biscuits to all of the dogs. Mo inhaled his and waited eagerly for another, but Robyn turned to another cupboard and took down a basket filled with every kind of tea imaginable, neatly labeled. "Pick your poison," she said. I pulled out a mint one.

Mo gave up on Robyn and wandered into the rest of the house. It must have passed inspection, because a couple of minutes later he reappeared and flopped to the floor at my feet with a grunt.

Robyn poured steaming water into two teacups that actually matched, ivy twining up their handles. All the mugs at home were a mishmash of souvenirs collected over the years. My favorite was the Tony the Tiger mug I'd gotten when my second-grade class toured the Kellogg's plant. It had a chip in it, but I'd keep it forever. Mom had been a parent chaperone on that trip.

Robyn eased onto the stool across the island. "I would like to have more dogs."

"Why don't you?"

"Oh, you know. Too expensive. Not enough space." Robyn tipped a spoonful of sugar into her cup and stirred. "The truth is, Lenny made me cut down."

I sipped my tea, and warmth curled through my stomach. "Who's Lenny?"

"My husband. I used to do a lot of fostering through the animal shelter, looking after abandoned dogs who needed special care until they could be adopted by a new family."

"Why would he have a problem with that?"

"Let's just say I would've been happy to adopt every dog myself."

"I can't imagine having more than one dog," I said. "Mo and I already trip all over each other."

"That was Len's complaint, too," she said. "And he wasn't wrong. This isn't a big house. But honestly, I think he was feeling a bit neglected. So we sat down, had a long talk, and compromised. I had Fontine from before we were married, and Oscar and Lorraine are two of my rescues."

"So you don't have any kids?" I asked.

"Just the furry kind." Robyn glanced at the clock on the wall. It was shaped like a black-and-white dog not unlike Mo, its tail wagging the time. "Come on now, we should get to work." She pushed back her stool. All four dogs leapt to attention. "Get the leash. Let's see how you're doing walking Mo."

Mo at my heel, I ventured deeper into the house than I really wanted to go. We walked past a bathroom, a master bedroom with bright country quilts piled on the bed, and a cave of a den with a bunch of cushions strewn on the floor. Robyn alternately praised and coached us. "Much better," she said. "Much, much better."

We started working on "sit" and "stay." Mo wasn't particularly good at either, or maybe I wasn't, but Robyn promised we'd get better with practice. It was funny how much energy I was willing to put into Mo. Mrs. Hoekstra, my chemistry teacher, would have been so jealous.

"You know," Robyn said as Mo and I got ready to leave, "I was thinking about your problem, leaving Mo alone all day."

"He's been really good lately. Mostly."

"Why don't you bring Mo by the clinic on your way

to school and pick him up on your way home?" When I hesitated, she added, "Free of charge, of course."

"I couldn't do that. You've done too much already."

"Oh, Lorraine, Oscar, and Fontine pretty much take care of each other during the day. Mo would love the company."

"I don't know," I said. Free surgery, free training, free day care—there had to be a catch.

"Tell you what. If you want to do something in return, you can clean up the poop in the yard and give them fresh water when you stop by."

Now that was a thrilling thought. Mo's poop was gross enough. Did I really want to deal with that times four? But at least then it wouldn't be something for nothing. I looked down at Mo, sitting at my feet, eagerly swishing his tail so I wouldn't forget to take him with me.

"Think it over," Robyn said, leaning down to pet him. "Consider it a standing invitation."

I did think it over, right there. I had to do what was best for Mo, whatever Robyn's reasons. "Thanks," I said. "We'll see you bright and early on Monday."

• • •

"Why does she care?" I asked Van on the phone that night. I slouched on the couch, TV on, empty soup bowl on the coffee table in front of me. Mo sat a few feet away, watching the bowl intently as if at any second it would fall on the carpet and become fair game.

I could hear Teddy babbling as Van thought it over. "Maybe she feels sorry for you," he said at last.

"Thanks a lot!"

"I'm giving you my honest opinion. She knows your mom's dead, your dad's away, you don't have much dough. You're nursing a three-legged dog back to health. And, to top it all off, you're short enough to be a Hobbit."

"You're lucky you're half a mile away or you'd be prying one pissed-off Hobbit's hands from your throat."

Mo gave up on the soup bowl and groped his way onto my lap. I stroked his neck. "I really don't want her pity."

"Well, does she have anything to offer that you *do* want? No, no, Teddy, that ring is attached to my ear. Let's keep it that way."

"She knows how to deal with this dumb mutt I've got."

"The way I see it—ouch, Teddy, cut it out!—the way I see it is, don't overanalyze things. She wants to help you, let her help you. She's not asking for anything in return, is she?"

"Just the poop," I said.

"That's it, Teddy, I've had it. Play with your blocks."

There was a rustle and a squawk of protest. Van came back on the line. "Speaking of asking for things, Col, I'm on the decorating committee for the AVD."

"The what?"

"The dance."

"Oh. Right. I keep thinking it stands for 'a venereal disease.'"

"Ha, ha. I was wondering if you wanted to help," Van said. "It's just me and Zak right now."

"I don't know if you've noticed, but I'm kind of boycotting the Alliance."

Van sighed. "I was afraid of that. Rachel and Michael, I assume?"

"Did you see the way he waltzed into our meeting like he's a charter member? And now he's invaded the Lounge! No place is sacred."

"I hate to break this to you, but nobody besides you is actually bothered by Michael being there. Most people seem to like him, in fact."

"People have to like him. He's Rachel's boyfriend and Mr. Newspaper Editor."

"Actually, I think they like him because he's nice," Van said. "Look, it sucks what happened to you, Col, but it's starting to sound like you're stuck on repeat."

"Fine. Go talk to Teddy. I'm sure he can offer far more stimulating conversation."

"Don't be a twit," Van said. "But check it: you claim you don't want the vet's pity, and here you are wallowing like a hippo in the mud."

"Thanks. I've always wanted to be compared to a three-thousand-pound jungle beast."

"You're welcome," he said. "Ooo, hey, what do you think about a jungle theme for the dance? It could be 'Get Wild' or something, and we could have green streamers hanging down from the ceiling like vines, and you could get your picture taken with Tarzan or Jane, and . . ."

I just shook my head and smiled as he rolled on. If my problem was wallowing, Van's was that he had the attention span of a hamster. Still, no amount of talking would change my mind about the dance—not when I knew Rachel and Michael would be there, pressed against each other while I stood alone.

**EACH MORNING I WOKE** up at an ungodly hour and took Mo for a jog. Back home, I snarfed a cup of coffee and a slice of toast. I drove Mo to the clinic, continued to school, tried to stay awake for the next six hours, then left and drove back to the vet's. First I picked up the poop, then my poop machine. Back home for homework and dinner. If I had work—work. Then back home for more homework, TV, walk, sleep, repeat.

As usual, Dad and I celebrated my birthday a few days early. That morning, over a breakfast of mushroom-cheese omelets and bacon, he asked where I wanted to go out to dinner. "The Grotto," I said. It was an Al Capone–themed pizza-and-burger joint by Western Michigan University.

"Bee, turning seventeen is pretty special. I thought we could go somewhere fancy for a change."

"The Grotto has the best pizza in town," I argued.

It was true; they served thick, tomato-covered, cheese-oozing, Chicago-style pizza that probably shouldn't be called pizza at all, it was so different from the cardboard crap in the frozen food aisle at Meijer. You needed a fork to eat it. But even more than that, there was no way I was going to squeeze into my only dress—the one I'd worn to Mom's funeral—just to eat overpriced food in a place where they looked at you cross-eyed if you used your forks in the wrong order.

"All right. It's your birthday. The Grotto it is." Dad dropped a scrap of bacon into Mo's gaping maw. "Anything on your wish list I can pick up for you?"

I pushed my eggs around on my plate, piling them into a sort of bird's nest. When I was little, I'd thought nothing about rattling off a dozen toys I wanted for my birthday, even though I knew, when the day rolled around, there would only be a couple. In middle school I'd chosen more carefully, writing down a short list of the things I wanted, adding at the bottom, "Any of these would be great." I'd wanted Mom and Dad to know I didn't expect them to buy everything, especially since we'd just had Christmas. I'd wanted them to know I understood we weren't rich and I didn't mind.

Then Mom died, and my wish list changed completely.

*How about giving up OTR trucking? Then maybe we'd have something to talk about besides whether Michigan or State has better defense and who's got the best fried rice in town.*

Ever since Dad told me about that trucker who gave up OTR, a small, stupid piece of me had been hoping the idea was flowering in Dad's mind, too. That he realized how tired he was of living on the road and how much he missed me, how being home would be worth any cut in pay. I'd gone so far as to imagine he'd come home on my actual birthday and tell me he'd quit his job.

"I could use some extra money," I said instead. "Scarlett's due for a tune-up."

Dad smiled. "Done! In fact, I'll take her in myself the next time I'm back. You've taken good care of her, Colby. I'm proud of you."

I tried to return his smile, but I felt like I'd requested an extra year of solitary confinement.

• • •

Dad let me invite Van along to The Grotto. The three of us devoured a steaming pie: half meat, half veggie for Van the Vegetarian. When the pizza was gone, we ordered a giant, gooey fudge brownie sundae to share.

"Thanks for dinner, Mr. B.," Van said as we waited for our dessert to arrive. "That was absolutely the most delicious thing I've put in my mouth all year."

I smirked, but Dad only thumped Van on the shoulder. "It's been real nice catching up with you. And I owed you one."

"Oh? Really?"

"Sure. I figure you deserve some credit for keeping Colby out of trouble while I'm gone."

"Trouble?" Van asked.

"Trouble?" I echoed.

"Boy trouble," Dad said. "You know how some guys are, barely able to keep it in their pants. If they saw an opportunity—"

Van choked on his root beer. "I don't know how much influence I have on Colby's love life, but I do try to help her with algebra."

"Thanks just the same. It's not that I think women are the weaker sex, but she's my little girl, you know?"

I locked eyes with Van, daring him not to laugh. He twitched with the effort. "Ten four, good buddy," he managed, landing an awkward punch on Dad's arm.

"You mean 'good neighbor,'" said Dad. "You call someone 'good buddy,' you're calling them a queer. Not, um, that there's anything wrong with that."

His red face said otherwise. This was the guy Van wanted me to come out to?

The waiter bustled by and, in the center of the table,

dumped three spoons and a huge porcelain clamshell heaped with mounds of vanilla ice cream, chunks of warm brownie, peaks of whipped cream, and a flood of molten fudge. We dug in wordlessly. But when I gave Van a sly smile, he had to look away to keep from busting up.

• • •

It was later, back home, that things went horribly wrong.

I was sprawled on the couch with Mo, starting to review for my history exam. Dad was sitting at our clunky old computer. And he said, "Colby, I've been thinking of truck shopping."

I went to the computer, Mo following. I assumed Dad meant another pickup, something to replace the ancient Chevy. Instead, he was looking at a website that sold big rigs.

"But what about SwifTrux, Dad? I thought you liked working for them."

"It's okay, sure. But as an owner-operator, I'd decide which jobs to take—when to work and where to go," Dad said. "Some O-Os gross hundreds of thousands a year. Besides, there's something about having wheels to call your own, know what I mean?"

Unfortunately, after having Scarlett, I knew exactly what he meant.

I stared at an ad for a rig with a cushy sleeping area.

The price made my forehead break out in sweat. "These are really expensive, Dad."

"I can finance a used one and make up the cost in a couple of years." He spoke so matter-of-factly that I could tell he'd been thinking about this for a while.

"Why now, Dad?" I asked. "What's changed?"

"Nothing's changed. Your mother and I discussed the idea years ago, but our finances weren't quite there. Now that things are"—he searched for the right word— "*stable* again, it seems like a good time."

Dad clicked another link on the site. "What do you think about this one?"

What did I think? A truck was a truck was a truck! "It looks like its face is mashed in."

He laughed. "It's a cab-over. The engine is underneath the seats. It's more space efficient than a conventional."

"Well, I think it's ugly." My mouth was dry. My stomach clenched up. I dug my fingers into the skin at the back of Mo's neck, and he whined.

If Dad bought his own rig, he was in this for good. Instead of getting a short-haul job, he'd keep working extralong weeks driving from one end of the country to the other. I'd come home each day with no one to talk to, no one to hug me, no one just to sit on the couch with who remembered and missed Mom the way I did. If Dad bought his own rig, my birthday wish would never, ever come true.

Dad clicked on a photo gallery of used rigs for sale. They came in just about every color, glossy and sleek and monstrous. Their headlights all stared at me blankly, like zombies. I felt like they were gnawing my heart out.

"Tell you what, Bee," Dad said, looking up at me. "Why don't you pick one out? What color do you think I should get?"

"Pink," I spat out. I didn't see a pink truck anywhere on the site. "Get pink."

"I can't get pink. I'd be laughed off the road. I don't even know if I could find one. Even lady drivers—"

"You said I could pick." I stared him down, my arms folded across my chest. "Promise you'll get pink, to remember me when you're on the road. That's the least you can do."

For a moment Dad looked—ashamed? Guilty? Both, I hoped. Then he sighed. "What if I got a white truck and painted it?"

"Doesn't count," I said, knowing exactly what would happen if I caved: he'd buy the first white rig he saw and find excuse after excuse not to get it painted. "Anyhow, after you spend a zillion dollars on a rig, how'll you pay for a decent paint job?"

"Well, I'll see what I can do."

"It's my birthday. I never ask you for anything anymore."

"I don't know why this is so important to you," Dad said, voice rising.

"Promise."

I didn't know why I bothered. Dad was going to do what he was going to do, and I had serious doubts that a guy who was bothered by getting called "good buddy" would actually drive a pink rig.

Dad shook his head, but he said, "All right, Colby. I promise."

**16**

**F**INALS WERE COMING up fast, and it felt like my teachers spent entire class periods rubbing in just how much I'd failed to learn over the semester. Meanwhile, I continued to plan my routes between classes to minimize sightings of Rachel and Michael gliding through the halls with their hands Super Glued together. It only worked some of the time.

And then, Friday afternoon, I found a strange girl waiting at my locker. She had long brown hair in a low ponytail that fell over her shoulder. Tortoiseshell glasses framed her face, and she wore a huge purple sweater and paisley skirt. She smelled faintly like peaches.

She smiled. "Colby Bingham."

"Yes?"

"Amelia," she said. When I shook my head, she added, "Amelia Hoogendoorn?"

"Right, sure," I said, even though the name meant nothing to me. Her face was vaguely familiar, but I couldn't say why.

"I'm on the staff of *The Watchman*."

"Okay. Cool." I spun the dial on my locker, opening the door with a bang.

"I wondered if I could interview you. For a feature on animal welfare. Michael—Michael Schmidt, the features editor?—he suggested I do one. About your dog."

I stopped shoving the night's load of homework into my backpack and stared. Forget peaches—I smelled a rat, a rat with the initials M. S. "What do you know about my dog?"

"Nothing. I mean, just what I heard from Rachel."

Make that two rats.

"That's interesting. I don't remember telling Rachel much of anything about my dog."

"Well, she got the whole story from Van."

Definitely time to call the exterminator.

I pulled on my coat and shut my locker. Amelia fell into step beside me as I headed for the back door. My brain clunked like a dryer full of sneakers. Amelia knew Michael from *The Watchman*. And if she knew

Michael, of course she'd know Rachel, too, since they were surgically attached these days. But how did she know Van?

"So, what do you think?" Amelia asked. "Can I interview you? It won't be on the front page or anything—I'm only a sophomore—but I think people would be really interested—you know, what you did for him—and maybe they'd drive more carefully—or, I don't know, something . . ." She trailed off.

I considered walking all the way out to Scarlett to see if she'd follow, but instead I paused at the door. She wasn't wearing a coat, and it was awfully cold outside. "All right, what the hell," I said. "I'll do it."

Her face lit up. "Great! How about Saturday?"

"Can't, I've got work. Sunday?"

"I've got a church thing. Sometime next week then. Monday?"

"Work again." This was getting ridiculous. "Tuesday?"

She grinned. "Tuesday it is!"

"But just so you know, I'll have to pick up my dog from the vet's first."

"Oh no! He isn't—"

Her concern surprised me. "He's okay," I said. "He just stays there while I'm at school. Long story."

"I could come with you," Amelia said. "We could pick him up and then go to your place and talk. Actually,

131

it would be better that way. I'll bring my camera and get some shots of your dog, maybe the road where he got hit, too." Her eyes were hopeful.

I shrugged. "If that's what you want. You know where my locker is."

• • •

Late that night, hours after Mo and I had come home from another training session at Robyn's, the doorbell rang. At this time of night it could only be the police. The door was the only barrier between me and the news that my dad was dead, thrown through his windshield when his rig jackknifed on an icy road in Bumblefuck, Minnesota. Or he got held up at a truck stop and got shot in the chest while heroically trying to save his cargo of five thousand lawn gnomes. Or—

The doorbell rang again, and over the noise of the basketball game on TV, I heard a muffled yell. "Col, open the door before Teddy and I get pneumonia!"

I flung it open. "What are you doing here?"

Van slid inside and plunked Teddy on the floor. Mo began washing the little guy's face. Teddy laughed and stuck out his own tongue. Great. Danielle would love that my garbage-eating, butt-sniffing mutt was swapping spit with her son.

Van shivered in his vest and blew on his fingers.

Twenty degrees outside, a half-mile walk, and he wasn't even wearing gloves out there. Idiot.

"Just thought we'd surprise you is all." He stooped to unzip Teddy's coat.

I shook my head and took the two steps into the kitchen to put on coffee—decaf; Van wouldn't drink the good stuff. "Carrying your baby nephew down Harrington Road on a dark, freezing night? What were you thinking?"

Van picked up Teddy again and wiped the dog slobber off with his shirttail. He sat at the table bouncing Teddy on his knee. I gave the kid my keys, which he inspected with great care before shaking and banging them on the table. Van finally answered the question: "Unexpected guests."

"Oh." Van's mom didn't have a steady boyfriend, but she'd been known to bring someone home without much warning. She didn't ask Van to make himself scarce, but the walls in his house were very, very thin. Still, "Why didn't you ask her for a ride?"

"I think they'd been at Happy Hour."

"Oh. Well. Next time, call me. I would've picked you up. Both of you."

"No car seat," Van pointed out.

"You could have become roadkill out there."

"We kept way to the side." But Van looked chagrined. He knew damn well that dogs and deer weren't the only casualties of Harrington Road.

I poured our coffee, and Van set Teddy and the keys on the floor, back within reach of Mo's tongue. Van wrapped his fingers around the mug—NUMBER ONE DAD!—to warm them.

"So," I said, "I got approached by a member of the press today."

"Ooo, let me guess! Is *National Geographic* doing a spread on the indigenous people of Trail's End?"

"No, it was *Cosmo*. They wanted celibacy tips and tricks. I gave them your number."

"Seriously."

"Seriously, it was someone from *The Watchman*. Amelia Something?"

A smile spread across Van's face. "Amelia Hoogendoorn?"

"So you do know her. Yeah. She wants to do an article on Mo."

"Awesome!" Van leaned over and knuckled Mo's mighty noggin. "This fella deserves to be famous."

"She said Michael asked her to do the article. How's that for weird? Actually, she said he got the idea from Rachel, who got the idea from you. Where do you know her from, anyway?"

"Oh, around. We have *la classe de français* together. Her French name is Amélie."

"Well, ooh la la. Do you know how chummy she is with Rachel and Michael? Because I don't need any of their BFFs butting into my life."

"It's not that big a school, Col. People know people. Not all of us are hermits."

"All right, all right. Forget it."

We moved to the couch, watching the end of the game as we waited for Danielle to swing by on her way home from work. Teddy fell asleep in Van's arms. We put a couch cushion on the floor, and Van laid Teddy on it. Mo slumped on the floor beside him, on guard duty, until his own head got too heavy. Mo rested his snout on the cushion beside Teddy. Soon they were snoring in harmony.

**17**

**B**Y THE TIME I packed up my bag on Tuesday afternoon, Amelia was standing at my elbow. She wore an ankle-length denim skirt, and this time her hair was loose and spilled onto her burgundy coat. In my usual jeans and sweatshirt, I felt a bit scruffy. What would Amelia think of my tinfoil house, my crippled mutt, and my redneck truck?

Out in the lot, I unlocked Scarlett's passenger door. "This is it," I said. I'd thrown out the trash that morning, but there was still white fur all over the place.

"It's so great you have your own car," Amelia said, hopping in. I slammed the door shut, then went around to let myself in. "I'll be lucky if my parents let me take driver's ed this summer. They've read too many statistics about how terrible teen drivers are."

"Do they know you're riding with a 'teen driver' today?"

"I told them you're very responsible and have never had an accident."

I snorted.

"You haven't, have you?"

"Not so far. I can't afford a hike in my insurance."

Amelia bombarded me with small talk all the way to the clinic. "Oh, I've seen this place," she said as we pulled in. "My aunt takes her cats here."

"What about you? Do you have pets?"

"Not really. Neil, my brother, has dwarf hamsters. I love animals, but our parents won't let us have anything big."

"My dad was the same way."

"Really? How'd you get him to change his mind?"

I grinned at her. "I didn't give him much of a choice."

Robyn was busy with patients, so we went straight to the backyard. Mo galloped over and put his muddy paws all over my jeans and Amelia's skirt. "Off!" I yelled, with zero success. The rest of the posse joined in, sniffing Amelia from all angles. "Sorry," I told her, dragging the dogs away by their collars.

"It's okay." She held out her hand for Mo to slurp. "Neil's hamsters never care if I'm around. It's nice to be greeted with so much— Aww, does the nice boy want his tummy rubbed? Oh yes, he does! Oh yes, he most certainly does!"

I had to appreciate her good taste in dogs. "Come on," I said to Amelia. "Let's get that interview out of the way." I'd pick up the poop tomorrow.

Amelia stood, and Mo stared up at us from the ground. When we turned to leave, he rolled himself upright and hurried along behind us, not about to be abandoned.

• • •

Amelia took Trail's End in stride. As I got us Cokes from the fridge, she took a short stroll around the living room. I was glad I'd vacuumed the crumbs from the couch cushions and stashed all the Christmas stuff back in Dad's closet. Mo followed her, waiting for more petting.

She paused at the framed photo hanging by the TV. It wasn't as if I ever forgot it was there, but most of the time I tried not to think about it. The photo was of Dad, Mom, and me, taken one afternoon on the boardwalk in South Haven when I was twelve. Back then Dad looked as fit as a quarterback in his souvenir Bears jersey. It's tough to stay in shape when you're behind the wheel all day, but he'd made the effort. I was scrawny in my bikini, my nose bright red with sunburn. And Mom—

well, Mom was beautiful, as always, her long, white-blond hair sweeping over her tan shoulder.

The most amazing thing was that we all looked so happy. Maybe because we were.

"Is that your mom?" Amelia asked.

I nodded. "My mom and dad."

"Wow. I can tell. You look just like her."

"Oh, please."

"No, really." Amelia cocked her head, looking at me, then the picture, then me again. "It's the color of your hair, of course, but it's more than that. Your eyes, maybe, or your mouth?"

"I don't know." Mom would always be taller, older, prettier. Well, not older. That was the awful thing—chances were that someday I'd be older than she was.

"Well, I meant it in a good way. She's beautiful."

"Was. She's dead." I remembered Rachel accusing me of never talking about Mom, so I added, "She had cancer."

"Oh, Colby."

I could see all the usual questions in her eyes: how long ago, was it sudden or slow, what kind of cancer—as if it mattered whether the tumors that killed you started in your gut or your brain or your boobs.

It was her skin: melanoma. And it happened both too slow and too fast. Too slow, because she had time to waste down to a walking skeleton, for that white-blond hair to fall out from chemo, for her legs to turn into a patchwork quilt of scars where she'd had tumors removed before she couldn't fight it anymore. Too fast, because I still wasn't ready to say good-bye.

But Amelia didn't ask any of those questions. She said, "I'm so sorry. You must miss her so much."

"Yeah." I turned away from the picture, headed for the couch, and cracked open a Coke, gulping. My eyes teared up, not just from the sting of bubbles in my throat. "Let's get started."

Amelia quietly sat at the opposite end of the couch and took a notebook and pen from her backpack. "Why don't you start with the first time you saw Mo?"

So I told her how Mo had barreled into my life. About the accident and the decision to adopt Mo that wasn't really a decision at all. About training him to be halfway civilized. About Robyn, who'd been as much fairy godmother as veterinarian from the very beginning. It was nice to have a story with a happy ending.

Mo insisted on sitting between us. He butted us whenever we weren't paying him enough attention.

"You know," Amelia said, setting her notebook on the coffee table and scratching Mo between the ears, "I've heard that a rescued animal will always be grateful to the person who saved it. That you can see it in their eyes."

"I don't know about that," I said. "Sounds like the kind of thing people say to feel better about themselves. What do you think?"

"Let me check." Amelia tipped her head toward Mo's and got an enthusiastic tongue across the face.

"Mo!" I scolded, but Amelia just laughed and took off her glasses, wiping the rest of her face with her sleeve.

"Do you have something I can clean these off with?"

I jumped up and retrieved a paper towel from the kitchen. "Sorry," I said.

"It's all right. Really. Congratulations, Mo, you've given me my first French kiss." She rubbed at one lens, then the other. Her face looked even softer without her glasses, except for her eyes. They might not see twenty-twenty, but they seemed as sharp as ever. They flickered up at me, and I looked away, embarrassed to have been caught staring. *Her first French kiss?*

Amelia put her glasses back on. "It's obvious he loves you, anyway."

"Well, dogs are supposed to love unconditionally, right?" I said. "No matter how many times you screw up. Lucky for me, huh, Mo? Considering the first thing I did was get your leg whacked off." I leaned over and kissed Mo on his cold, black nose. "Sorry about that."

Amelia took her camera out of her bag and snapped some shots of Mo sitting on the couch. I didn't like the thought of the entire student body knowing just how unglamorous my living room was, but I was too embarrassed to say so.

"Now some with you," Amelia said.

I put my hands up to my hair, my shabby sweat-shirt. "I don't think—"

"You look fine," she said.

"Fine?" I repeated.

"You look good," she said quickly. "And I promise to use only flattering photos."

I still went to change my shirt and fix my hair.

"Beautiful," Amelia said when I returned.

That word again. My stomach did a cartwheel. "Okay," I said, pretending I hadn't heard. "Where do you want me?"

Amelia took some photos of me with my arm around Mo. Mo and me sprawled on the floor, wrestling. Mo and me playing tug-of-war with his rope toy.

"You know," Amelia said, setting her camera on the coffee table, "it's funny."

I glanced up from the carpet where I was giving Mo a tummy rub. "What?"

"Last week when I asked you for this interview? You

were, um, not the most approachable person."

I focused on scratching Mo's not-so-bony-anymore ribs, and he wriggled and mooed in pleasure. "Van says I do a very convincing cactus impression."

"That's the thing . . . Right now? You're totally different. You're so sweet with Mo. So . . . um. I was surprised, I guess."

I slapped Mo on the rump. He jumped to his feet and attacked one of his chew toys. I sat back on the couch beside Amelia. "School's not exactly the place for sweetness. That's part of my secret identity." I half smiled to let her know I was kidding—sort of.

Amelia smiled back. She had dimples in her cheeks. "I won't tell anyone."

"Good. Because there'll be trouble if the truth gets out."

"Really? What kind of trouble?"

"Big trouble."

"Like what?"

I was about to open my mouth again, let the first stupid thing that came to mind spill out, but I stopped. Her smile, this teasing—she barely knew me, and I knew even less about her. Now that the interview was over, we'd go back to our separate corners of Westnedge High and never speak to each other again. She was just being nice. The last thing I needed was for my heart to get broken again by another girl who'd dump me the second the right guy made his move. I'd rather stick to my lonely-girl-and-her-dog existence.

I kept my mouth shut.

Amelia picked up her camera and fiddled with it. "I know what you mean. Feeling like a completely different person, depending on where you are, who you're with. The whole double-life thing."

"Right," I said. "I'll bet you have some really deep secrets to hide." I meant the words to be light, but they came out angry instead.

Amelia glanced at her watch. "Um, well, I'd better call my dad. It's almost six. Can I use your cell? One more thing my parents won't let me have."

How could so much time have passed? But then my stomach growled, and I realized it was dark outside. "I'll give you a ride," I said. "If that's okay with you."

"Of course it's okay."

I gave Mo a treat and promised him a good, long walk when I returned. Then Amelia and I hopped in Scarlett and headed back toward town.

Amelia's neighborhood wasn't as fancy as Rachel's. It was all ranches and split-levels with one-car garages, but it was still a big step up from Trail's End. When we pulled up to her house, she reached out and squeezed my arm, and I felt a gentle but unmistakable current pass between us. *Stop*, I told myself. *Don't even go there.*

"Thanks again for the interview," she said. "I'll see you at school, okay?"

I stared after Amelia until she got safely inside, trying not to think about the last time I'd dropped off a girl. There was a lingering scent of peach in the cab. I knew I'd smell it on the couch, too, when I got home.

**18**

**W**E HAD FINALS the rest of the week, two per day, and they were every bit as bad as I expected. Well, I did all right in English. History and Spanish weren't great, but I'd pass. The same with algebra, thanks to a last-minute cram session with Van. And I'd get at least a B in phys ed; anyone who put in a drop of effort did. But I knew that even the world's most generous curve wouldn't bring me up to a D in chemistry.

By Friday night I was desperate to get to Robyn's just so I could stop imagining what method Dad would use to kill me when he saw my grades. Once again Mo and I climbed the stairs to Robyn's place, and the door swung open before I could knock. She was wearing her Lions sweat suit again, too.

"I hate to tell you this," I said, "but the Lions sucked this season."

She laughed. "When don't they? But you've got to root for the home team."

"I don't. Go, Bears!"

"Oh, come in, you traitor."

Robyn already had the kettle on. I sat at the island while Mo and the other dogs went through their sniffing ritual. Oscar, the fuzz ball, ran into the living room and returned with a rubber cat. He and Mo tussled, the cat squeaking feebly every time it changed jaws.

"How's school going?" Robyn asked as we sipped our tea.

I shrugged. No way was I mentioning finals. "Not exactly my favorite pastime, but I'm dealing."

Robyn nodded. "I always liked school—the academic parts, I mean—but it was my friends who really made it all worthwhile."

I grimaced. My supply of friends had dwindled lately without soccer or the Alliance. When it came down to it, the only friend I could really count on was Van. And Mo. I stretched out a leg and stroked his back with my foot. He flicked his eyes up to mine, then closed them, sighing noisily.

"I grew up around here, too," Robyn said, "over by WMU. But I went to State for veterinary school. They have a great program. I was one of those kids who knew what they wanted to be in kindergarten. When I was six, I had a worm hospital."

"Excuse me?" I sputtered.

Robyn laughed. "After a rainstorm I'd walk around the neighborhood and scoop up all the worms that were half dried out on the sidewalk. I'd put them in a shoe box full of wet grass and dirt until they were healthy enough to put in the yard . . . or until they died."

"What did your parents think?"

"Oh, they thought it was cute, in a weird way. My mother said she couldn't wait until I had children of my own, to see what kind of bizarre things they did." Robyn smiled wryly. "What about you, Colby? What are your plans for the future?"

"I'll probably be bagging groceries till I'm ninety. Or, if I'm lucky, I'll make cashier by fifty." I laughed. Robyn didn't. I held my teacup close to my face, hiding behind the steam, and asked, "What's your husband do?"

"He works at a furniture factory near the Indiana border. It's a long day there. I think I'm on my feet a lot, but Lenny says I don't know how good I've got it."

"My dad sits all day. He says his butt is one giant callus."

"I don't think you ever told me what he does."

"He drives trucks OTR. Over the road. Cross-country."

"Ah."

I gulped the rest of my tea and pushed the cup away, refusing to meet Robyn's sympathetic eyes. "Come on, Mo," I said, poking him in the ribs with my toe. "Time to get to work."

We worked on "watch me" and "touch," to bring Mo's attention from whatever he was fixated on back to me. When I said "Watch me" and pointed to my eye, he was supposed to make eye contact. It sounded simple, but it wasn't once Robyn brought a squeaky toy, a stinky liver treat, or another dog into the picture—all of which trumped boring old me.

"Touch" was easier, and it melted my heart every time. I'd hold out the palm of my hand and say, "Touch!" Mo would stretch out his neck and touch his cold, wet nose to my palm. Sometimes he even added a little lick, but that was probably because my hands stank of liver treats.

We were still working when the kitchen door swung open and a draft chilled our ankles. All four dogs scurried to investigate. Heavy footsteps crossed the linoleum. It was a dark-haired, broad-shouldered guy wearing scuffed leather work boots and worn, baggy jeans. His light-blue shirt had a red-and-white plastic name tag pinned to the chest that read L. VOORHEES. Lenny.

"Hi, sweetie," Robyn said, pecking his cheek. "You're home early."

"They did another round of layoffs today," he said.

"Guess who didn't make the cut?"

"Oh, Lenny, I'm so sorry." She wrapped her arms around him. "Don't worry. You'll find something else, and we'll manage in the meantime. Everything will be okay."

Mo sniffed Lenny's boots. "Sorry. I didn't realize we had company," he said.

"Oh, for heaven's sake, where are my manners?" Robyn said. "Colby, this is my husband, Lenny. Lenny, this is Colby Bingham and Mo, the adorable tripod dog I was telling you about."

"Hi," I said awkwardly.

"Nice to meet you." Lenny shook my hand, but it was clear that his mind wasn't on me. He turned back to Robyn. "I'm going to shower. We can talk later, I guess."

Robyn squeezed his arm as he brushed past us. "Don't worry about it, Len. We'll work it out somehow," she called just before the bathroom door slammed shut.

"I should get home," I said.

Robyn didn't argue. We walked through the kitchen, Mo trooping faithfully behind us. He kept looking down the hallway where Lenny had disappeared—maybe wondering why he hadn't received a friendly pat from the stranger.

"See you next Friday?" Robyn asked as I slid into my coat.

"You're sure? We don't have to if things are—"

"Colby, the factory's been having trouble for years now, so what happened today is hardly a surprise. Besides, if Lenny and I treated every rough patch as the end of the world, we'd never have made it a week together, much less ten years." Robyn pulled on her own coat. "We'll meet next Friday, and everything will be back to normal, all right? Come on, I'll walk you out."

The six of us—two humans, four dogs—thumped down the stairs into the yard. The dogs trotted around in the slush and mud.

Robyn said, "This isn't the first time Lenny's been laid off, but he always takes it so hard."

"Will you really be all right?" I asked. "Because maybe I could start paying for—"

"Nonsense," Robyn said. "We'll be fine. And, Colby, I would never accept money for these little lessons. Mo's my patient, but I'd rather have you as a friend. Okay?"

I nodded. Robyn had to be at least twice my age, but I figured I should take any friend I could get.

**19**

**From the Rainbow Alliance Internet Lounge:**

**schmitty:** Did everyone see The Watchman article about the AVD? Absofreakinlutely brilliant.

**writergrrl:** *blushes* Thanks for publishing it. The posters are really great, too.

**stonebutterfly:** Aw, shucks. Anyone want to help me flyer this weekend?

**rachel_greenbean:** I'll go.

**schmitty:** Me, too.

**el_suavo:** Me, three.

**van_the_man:** I can't believe nobody likes my jungle theme idea.

**van_the_man:** Or my arctic theme. Hello, it is freaking freezing outside, i.e. perfect!!!

**z-dawg:** Face it, bro, nobody wants to dance in parkas and mukluks.

**van_the_man:** You could dress as a penguin.

**kittykat96:** I for one would like NORMAL things. Hearts and cupids and candy, kplsthnx.

**yinyang:** I gotta go with Liliana on this one.

**writergrrl:** Sorry, me too.

**van_the_man:** You are all unbelievably boring.

• • •

Second semester began on a low note—specifically, a note from the guidance office. Mrs. Hoekstra had notified my counselor that taking Chemistry 2 probably wasn't in my best interest. Instead, I'd have study hall.

The catch was that I couldn't just eat the F if I wanted my state-endorsed diploma next year. That meant I had a totally rockin' summer ahead of me, taking both Chem 1 and 2. The only thing worse would be sticking around Westnedge High for a fifth year.

I saved all our mail that week, even the ads for laser eye surgery and a coupon for a maternity shop. I wanted there to be plenty of camouflage for my report card by the time Dad came home.

When the dreaded moment arrived, I was washing the breakfast dishes. Dad turned on the TV to a show about the Great Wall of China, then picked up the stack of mail and began flipping through it. I watched out of the corner of my eye as he got closer and closer to the bottom and bit my lip as he slid his thumb under the flap of the envelope.

His brow furrowed as he scanned the page. "Colby," he said in a voice that wasn't angry or disappointed or anything at all. An empty voice. Somehow, Mo took it as his cue to run over, tail wagging, and put a paw in Dad's lap.

I set down the pan I'd been scouring, slowly dried my hands on the dish towel, and walked into the living room. I looked past him, through the curtains at the gloomy sky. "Yeah?"

"Am I reading this right? You failed chemistry?"

"Sort of," I muttered. "I have to retake it before I can graduate."

"What's going on, Colby? Do I have to send you back to Aunt Sue's so she can put you under house arrest?"

"I'll do better this semester."

"You're right, you will. How are you going to get into college if you're failing out?"

I didn't state the obvious.

"Bs and Cs are one thing. Even a D—okay, I get it,

nobody's a genius at everything. But an F! Bee, this arrangement we have, we've each got responsibilities. And school—"

"Relax, Dad," I said. "It's one lousy class. It's not like I want to be a chemist or whatever."

"You're so smart. If you'd just buckle down—"

"I know. I'm sorry."

"Sorry doesn't cut it! Sorry doesn't change that grade! Goddammit, you used to do *well* in school—" He glared at the TV, at that wall that went on for miles and miles, that once upon a time meant something but now only separated nothing from nothing.

We both knew what had changed. I'd done fine in middle school, even spending a few semesters on the honor roll. Then Mom got sick. Things that used to be as easy as breathing, like brushing my teeth or making toast, were suddenly a struggle. Even breathing wasn't easy sometimes. How could I sit through six hours of class every day? How could I remember Civil War battlefields or identify a metamorphic rock?

And after she died it only got worse.

I stooped, grabbed one of Mo's toys, and tossed it. Mo tackled it and shook it so forcefully that it made me dizzy. My report card dangled from Dad's hand like a feeble white flag.

**20**

**"SO, THIS SKELETON** walks into a bar. He says, 'Bartender! I'd like a beer and a mop!'"

It took a second for me to get it as I pulled out of the McIneanys' driveway. Then, "Ha. Ha. Ha."

"Oh, come on!" Van protested. "It's funny!"

"Another Peabody Special?"

"How'd you guess?"

"You and Mr. P. are peas in a pod."

"I think you mean peas in a Peabody. Alliance boycott or not, you really ought to stop by and see him." Van broke off half of his granola bar and passed it back to Mo, who wolfed it down. "He always asks about you."

"Tell him there are far more important things to worry about than me," I said.

But Van was right: I really ought to stop by Mr. P.'s room and say hi. It was Mr. Peabody who'd persuaded me to join the Alliance in the first place, fall of sophomore year. Word had been getting around that I was gay, and while I'd never been especially popular, I'd never had other kids throw Coke cans at my head or whisper nasty things about me in the locker room, either. The aura of grief that had protected me after Mom died was fading. Now I was fair game.

I don't know whether Van had told Mr. P. that I was having a hard time or if he'd found out the way everyone else seemed to, but one day he kept me after English and put an Alliance flyer in my hands. "Come to a meeting—just one—before you decide," he'd said in response to the skeptical look on my face. "Who knows? You might just meet the lady of your dreams."

"Hey," Van said. "Guess who else asked about you?"

I held my breath as we sped north on Harrington Road. "Rachel?"

"Oh, Col. We've talked about this obsession five thousand times."

No comment. I flipped on my blinker and turned into the clinic lot.

"It was Amelia. Ameeeeelia Hooooogendoorn!" Van sang her name as if he were on Broadway.

"Oh. Her." I felt a flutter in my stomach but didn't

want to give Van the satisfaction of seeing my interest. I put Scarlett in park, leaving the engine running. It was another bone-chilling day.

"She asked if I'd seen you. She said she has something to show you."

"It's probably just stuff for her *Watchman* article." What with finals and Dad's freak-out, I'd pretty much forgotten about it.

"You never really told me how the interview went," Van said.

"You'll see for yourself when it comes out."

"Not that—I meant her. You. What did you think of her?"

I threw open my door and ushered Mo out. "She seemed nice," I said carefully. "Why?"

"No reason," Van said with a grin. "I think she is, too."

• • •

After school Amelia was waiting at my locker with a handful of papers. She smiled so brightly, I felt the corners of my own mouth tug upward, but I forced myself to stay cool. "How's it going?"

"I wanted to show you the proofs for the article. *The Watchman* goes to press tomorrow." She peeled off the top couple of sheets and handed them to me.

*Student Gives Stray a Second Shot at Life*

*Colby Bingham wasn't expecting a reward when she and fellow junior Donovan McIneany saved a stray dog hit by a car on Harrington Road this past December 22nd. "I barely even know first aid," says Bingham. "I just knew I had to do something." But she didn't know how many difficult decisions lay ahead. . . .*

I scanned the rest of the article: what went down at the clinic, Mo's road to recovery, stats on the number of strays in Kalamazoo County, the dangerous conditions on Harrington Road. She hadn't turned the story into a tabloid tearjerker. She'd quoted me honestly and stated the facts. I liked that.

Then there was the photo of Mo and me. Mo was crouched in anticipation as I held his favorite chew toy in front of his nose. Amelia had taken the photo on Mo's right side, so you got the full glory of his missing leg.

"Well?" Amelia asked nervously when I handed back the proofs.

I nodded. "Looks good."

"Great! That's what was most important to me." She brushed a strand of hair away from her face and smiled again. "I printed out some extra photos of you and Mo, if you want them."

I flipped through them. In each, Mo looked like a total sloppy-tongued spaz—no surprise there. What startled me was how *I* looked. I looked happy. I looked like Van had just told me the corniest joke in the entire history of corny jokes, but I was still laughing because nothing in the world could ruin my good mood. I hadn't seen myself looking so happy in a long, long time.

"Thanks. I'd love to have them."

I expected her to go, but she didn't. She leaned against the locker beside mine, her papers clutched to her chest, and waited. Loitered, you might say. *Lingered*.

I packed my bag and put on my coat. The hallway was just about empty now. Soon we'd be alone. "Well," I said, "I should probably go find Van. I guess I'll see you around." I started to move away.

"Wait, Colby!"

I stopped so quickly, my shoes squeaked on the tiled floor.

"I was, uh, I was wondering if maybe you'd want to get together sometime."

"You mean, just to hang out?"

"Yes. No. Sort of." Her cheeks had turned into strawberries. "Oh, God, I'm making a mess of this."

I stared at her. She couldn't be going where I thought she was going.

She stumbled on. "I used to try and catch your eye at Alliance meetings, back before you quit. I thought you were cute and funny, but you never noticed me, and I was too shy to say anything. But I always thought if we had the chance to talk— That's why I was so excited when Michael asked me to do the article about your dog. I thought it would be the perfect— Though I did have second thoughts when you were so— But then you turned out to be—" She broke off. "I'm sorry. I'm really nervous, if that's not completely obvious."

Amelia had noticed *me*? She'd tried to catch *my* eye? No one had ever chased me before. I never knew it could make your brain spin in ten different directions at once.

I flashed back to when I was the one clambering for Rachel's attention. I'd seen her around school, but we'd come from different parts of town, different crowds; we might as well have come from different planets. It had taken weeks for Van and me to worm our way into her life, and weeks more of my pushing and prodding, courting her, getting her to open up, zigzagging precariously toward that moment in the park when I first kissed her.

And I'd finally made it. For all the good it did me in the end.

"I didn't know you were in the Alliance," I said, though I remembered thinking her face *had* been hazily familiar. "Why didn't you say so before?"

"I just joined in the fall. And when it was clear you didn't recognize me in the slightest, well"—Amelia blushed even harder—"I was too embarrassed to bring it up. It's not like it's *that* big a group, you know?"

"So you're gay."

"I'm kind of avoiding labels. I know I like girls, but I'm not ready to write off guys, either."

"You're writergrrl," I said, finally matching the faceless online identity with this girl in front of me: silky brown bun pinned up with Number Two pencils, eager hazel eyes behind the tortoiseshell frames, long-fingered hands gripping her papers. "Your parents don't know about you."

Her eyes flashed. "I'm hardly the only one. But yes."

"Then who *does* know?"

"My friends know I'm in the Alliance. Some of them, anyway—the ones I can trust. My parents think I'm at Eco Club. As long as I bring home tips about recycling and conserving energy, they don't ask questions."

I shook my head, still reeling. Sure, I'd felt something the day of the interview, but I'd assumed it was coming from me, not her.

"What if I say yes?" I asked, stalling. "What happens if it gets back to your parents? What happens when it gets hard? Are you going to tell them the truth? Or are you going to ditch me and decide you'd rather stick to boys after all?"

"I'm sorry," Amelia said quietly. "I really wish I could come out like you, not caring what anyone else thinks. But I can't. I can't live in my parents' house for the next three years knowing that every time they look at me, they feel pity or disgust or hate or guilt or confusion or any of those other things I know they'd feel. And they'd try to convince me *I'm* confused and take me to our pastor and pray that I'll change and—"

I put my hand on her arm. "Stop. Please stop."

Why was I putting her through this? Why didn't I just say "Sure, whatever, let's make out at my place"? And I could take off her glasses and bury my face in her peach-scented hair and see the body she hid under those mounds of sweaters. I could feel that connection again, that sensation of someone reaching past my walls to get at the person inside.

But it didn't matter. Liking her wasn't enough. Say I opened up to her, fell hard, and then things went wrong—and things always went wrong. My heart was still littered with the rubble that Hurricane Rachel left in its wake. I couldn't risk another disaster.

"Look," I said, "I'm flattered, really, but I just don't think it'll work out."

Then I turned away before those hazel eyes could change my mind.

**21**

**"YOU DID WHAT?"** Van screeched.

Five minutes later we were sitting in Scarlett, dead last in line to get out of the parking lot. I'd found him by the back door, copying out his math homework to sell to some sad cheat with disposable income. "You get asked out by a girl who's pretty and smart, and you turn her down?"

"You don't understand," I said. Scarlett lurched forward another car length. *Why* did I tell him?

"She asked you out on one date."

"Yes, but she's—"

"Don't you dare say it's because she's not Rachel. I'm sick of hearing about Rachel. She never gave as good as she got when it came to you."

"Why would things be any better with Amelia?" I asked, finally pulling out of the lot.

Van scowled. "You know she likes you. That seems like a good start to me."

"But she's a closet case. Her parents don't know—"

"You hassled Amelia over *that*? Oh, that's rich, unless you've had the big conversation with your dad and just haven't told me yet."

Now it was my turn to scowl. "It's different," I said. "My dad is never around."

"That's got to be the lamest excuse I've ever heard! Like you haven't had a hundred chances to tell him. Just admit you're scared, Colby. Like everybody is. Like Amelia is."

"All right. I wasn't fair to her. How can you stand being friends with such a bitch?"

"It's just . . . I would have said yes in a second," Van said softly. "Amelia practically handed herself to you on a silver platter. Uh, so to speak."

"Remember when Robyn said Mo's leg was beyond repair?" I asked. "Face it, that's me."

"Except Mo's happy as a clam, and you're anything but," Van pointed out. "Robyn whacks off his leg, and it's like nothing bad ever happened to him."

"My heart isn't a leg. I can't just whack it off."

Van sighed. "I know."

I parked with a jolt outside the clinic. Van stayed in the truck while I cleaned up the yard. Mo didn't know what to make of my silence. He kept coming up to me, whining and licking my hand until it was raw and frozen. I was so tired of the ache I got in my chest when I thought of Rachel. Why couldn't my life be as simple as Mo's?

Back in Scarlett, heading home, I turned to Van. "What do I do now?"

Van scratched Mo behind the ears. "Glad you asked. You've got to call her. Apologize. Amelia's too nice to leave things like this."

"Okay. But what do I say about—"

"You can still tell her no. It's a free country."

"I know. But should I?"

"I'll put it this way: if it were me, I'd be kneeling before her, kissing her feet."

"Oh, come on. If it were you, you'd be doing a lot more than—"

Van grinned. "Some things go without saying. But seriously, do you want to go out with her? I mean, you said she's nice, but do you *like* her? Because there's no point in saying yes if you don't."

"I don't know if I *like* her right now," I said, "but I feel like I probably could."

"If you gave yourself the chance."

"Yeah. Something like that." I turned into the McIneanys' driveway and put Scarlett in park. She purred like a two-ton kitten. "Van, why didn't you tell me you knew Amelia from the Alliance? She completely blindsided me."

"Because every once in a while," Van said, giving Mo a final pat on the head, "getting blindsided can be a good thing."

• • •

I called Amelia that night before I lost my nerve. Van, unable to stay out of my business for more than five minutes at a time, had texted her number to me as soon as I got home.

A woman answered. Her mother?

"May I speak to Amelia?"

"Who is calling, please?"

"Colby Bingham. From school."

"One moment." As the phone was set down, I heard the buzz of a house with actual people in it: footsteps, voices, music. On my end it was just Mo and me breathing. I'd turned off the TV. I couldn't have any distractions.

At last there was a click. "Um, hello?"

"Hi, Amelia. It's Colby. I wanted—"

"Hold on—Mom, did you hang up the other phone?" Seconds passed, and the buzz turned to silence.

"Okay," Amelia said, her voice as clear as if she were sitting beside me, leaning in close.

I dug my fingers into Mo's ruff for support. "I'm sorry for being a jerk earlier."

There was a pause. Finally, Amelia said, "I really felt like a moron, you know? I was so mad! At myself, really, for getting my hopes up—"

"I get it. I'm pretty familiar with that feeling, too."

"So we can pretend this never happened?"

"Sure." She was giving me an out, letting me walk away—forget her. But . . . if she'd give me a second chance, I was going to take it. "Listen, do you still want to get together sometime?"

"You're, um, serious?"

"I'm serious."

"What I said about my parents? That's not going to change. Not any time soon."

"It's all right. Besides, sneaking around can be fun."

She laughed. I hugged Mo so hard he groaned like an old accordion.

"The thing is, Amelia . . . I'm kind of a mess. I think it would be better for both of us if we take things slow, don't rush into anything—you know?"

"There's that dance on Saturday, the one the Alliance is planning," Amelia said as if she hadn't heard. "I'd really like to go."

• • •

Van cornered me outside the cafeteria during lunch the next day. "You talked to Amelia!"

I stared up at the brown water stains in the ceiling tiles. "Hey, Van, look at that spot up there. Don't you think it looks like a rabbit? Wearing a beret? And holding a tennis racket?"

"Yeah, yeah, you're hilarious. I know you talked to Amelia!"

"Did she say something?" Who else knew?

"She didn't have to say anything," Van said. "I passed her in the hall, and I could tell by the look she gave me. I can't believe you didn't say anything this morning. You have got to tell me what's going on!"

"Oh, nothing, really."

"Colby Bingham!"

"Okay, okay!" I gave him a quick summary.

Van was the best cheerleader a friend could have. He jumped up and down. He wanted to pick out my outfit for Saturday. He had a restaurant in mind. He wanted me to try the breath-freshening spray he'd picked up at Walgreens. He seemed to think asking Amelia out was the best thing I'd done in my life—which maybe, given my track record, wasn't that far off.

**22**

**SATURDAY NIGHT** I pulled up to the curb at Amelia's place. She emerged, skipped to the truck, and let herself in, cheeks glowing. Her hair was combed away from her face and fastened with a delicate gold barrette, but long, loose strands had slipped free at her temples. Even though her parents were probably watching from the house, or maybe *because* they were watching, I had the sudden urge to touch her, to stroke those strands behind her ears, to unzip her bulky, burgundy coat to see what she was wearing underneath.

"Where are we going tonight?" I asked. "As far as your parents know, I mean."

Amelia laughed dryly. "Seeing a documentary about global warming for Eco Club."

"Wow. It'll be hard to top that for fun, but we can try."

We drove to a Middle Eastern restaurant up near Western that Van had insisted we try. It felt so good to have a girl riding shotgun again—*my* girl, if only for the night.

We slid out of our coats at the restaurant. Amelia was wearing a long skirt (of course) swirled with purple and brown, and a cream-colored peasant's blouse with a neckline that scooped *almost* low enough to show the tops of her breasts. "You look really great," I told her.

She blushed. "You, too. Your eyes look so blue."

"I'll tell Van. He'll say, 'I told you so.'" I'd been all set to wear one of my trusty pink pullovers, but Van—who'd come over for a last-minute intervention—had dug into the back of my closet and pulled out a sky-blue sweater with silver thread woven in. It had been a gift from Aunt Sue, and I'd never bothered to take off the tags. But it actually looked pretty good on me.

We ordered stuffed grape leaves and shish kebab, which the waiter brought on sizzling, black, iron plates. Amelia told me about her favorite class, journalism, and how she played clarinet in concert band and sang in her church choir. I told her I liked English and history best (though it was sort of like picking your favorite disease) and that I used to play soccer.

171

"Why'd you stop?"

I carefully rearranged the smoky chunks of chicken, tomato, and bell pepper into a ring on my plate. "My mom died halfway through the season freshman year."

"Oh, Colby."

"I wasn't good for much, so I quit. And I didn't even bother trying out sophomore year."

"Why not?"

"I guess it just didn't seem that important anymore. I mean, it's soccer. You can run around and score goals all day, but it's not like it'll change the world. It's not like it'll change anything."

We were silent a moment. Conversation killed once again with the Dead Mother Technique. Then Amelia said, "I think you should go back and play."

"Nah. I've got my hands full. School. Work. Mo. The Lady Wolves were conference champs last year. They don't need me, and there's no way I could make the time commitment."

"You could play in one of the summer leagues."

I shook my head. "More work. And more school. I've got to retake chemistry. Apparently, my whole life will be meaningless if I don't pass it."

I waited for Amelia to tell me that, actually, my life *would* be meaningless if I didn't pass chemistry. Instead she said, "It's funny, isn't it, all the things we've got to do to graduate. Like, did you take PE with Mr. Crabtree? We had a whole unit on jump roping last semester. *Jump roping*. I can't believe 20 percent of my grade depended on whether I could hop up and down while swinging a rope."

"Right," I said, "like someday you're going to interview for a job, and they're going to ask you to do a crisscross or double-jump. Ditto square dancing. In what real-world situation will I ever have to allemande left?"

"It's an integral part of our cultural history and encourages positive social interactions," Amelia droned. Then she winked at me. "Or so Mr. Crabtree says."

I grinned, thinking, *Thank you. Thank you for not pushing the soccer issue or my chemistry grade. Thank you for not telling me to get over Mom.*

I drove one-handed to school, my other hand entwined with Amelia's. She looked way too happy about this simple hand-holding. But then, maybe I did, too.

• • •

The dance had already started by the time we arrived. Amelia and I held hands as we edged into the cafeteria. Red and pink garlands hung from every available surface. There was a huge, heart-shaped wreath of balloons where you and your date could get your photo taken, plus a table with a bowl full of pink punch and mounds of heart-shaped cookies. A disco ball was tacked to the ceiling. There wasn't a vine or iceberg in sight (much to Van's disappointment, I was sure).

Mr. Peabody greeted us at the door. His bald spot blinked green, blue, and red as the lights overhead flashed and spun. "*Colby* Bingham! *Amelia* Hoogendoorn!"

"*Mr.* Peabody!" Amelia exclaimed.

He beamed. "May I just say, nothing could thrill me more than to see two of my favorite young people taking notice of each other?"

"Permission granted," Amelia said, then nudged me. "Colby?"

I hoped if anyone saw how pink my face was, they'd think it was from the lights. "Yeah, sure. Though, no offense, Mr. P., if nothing could thrill you more, I think you need to get out a little more often."

He patted me on the shoulder. "I've missed your acid wit, Colby. Welcome back to the world. Now, get out there, girls, and boogie down."

"He's so sweet, isn't he?" Amelia said, laughing, as we walked away.

"He's the biggest nerd I've ever met," I said, "but also the best."

We cruised around the room, dancing with Liliana and Zak and other kids from the Alliance. They smiled in recognition that Amelia and I were here together, like *together*. I wanted everyone to know I was here with Amelia—that Colby Bingham was on an honest-to-goodness date with an honest-to-goodness girl. That I was totally over Rachel.

I caught sight of Van, bopping by on the arm of some guy, then another guy. When Amelia's head was turned, he made a V with his fingers and wiggled his tongue between them. I flipped him the bird. He laughed and danced away.

Then the music slowed, the beat fading into a sappy ballad. Amelia put her hands around my shoulders, I put my hands on her waist, and I marveled that there really was a waist under those bulky sweaters, and it was soft and curvy. For the next slow song, she put her hands on *my* waist, and I stepped in close, wrapped my arms around her, and laid my head on her shoulder. I heard her heart thundering under my ear, and I smiled.

I couldn't help wondering how far she'd go with me.

Behind my closed eyelids I saw Rachel, the one and only time I kissed her bare breasts. She was so flat, she wore boys' tank tops instead of bras. It had been so easy to push up the shirt to her armpits and put my mouth on what was underneath. And she let me, that time. She gasped and dug her fingers into my arms. She told me not to stop when I asked her if I should. But the next time she'd stopped me for good. She'd never so much as unhooked my bra, much less kissed my breasts. Would Amelia? Ever?

I broke away at the next fast song. "Want a drink?"

Amelia nodded, breathless. We headed for the punch bowl, and I ladled pink sugar water into two cups.

And that's when I spotted Rachel and Michael, dancing.

I shouldn't have been surprised. It figured the regular Valentine's Dance wasn't enough for them. They just *had* to be supportive, had to keep reminding me of what I'd lost. Rachel wasn't wearing a dress, of course—if she and Michael went to prom, they'd probably both wear tuxes—but she managed to look radiant in her khakis and olive V-necked sweater. All that radiance was aimed directly at Michael, and he radiated right back.

And for the first time, I truly believed that Rachel was going out with Michael not to make her parents happy, not because it was easier than going out with girls in general or me in particular, but because she loved him.

I tore my gaze away and set down my punch on the table. Amelia leaned close and whispered, "You okay?"

There was a strange, heavy feeling in my stomach. Not bad-strange, exactly, just strange-strange. It was like all this time there had been a door between Rachel and me, open just a crack, and I'd been breaking my fingernails trying to pull it wider. And it had finally slammed shut for good. *Maybe someday* had become *never*, and it was kind of a relief.

I slipped an arm around Amelia's waist and squeezed. "Come on. Let's dance some more."

"You've got it," she said. "We can practice our allemande left."

I was disappointed when, a while later, Amelia glanced at her watch, put her lips near my ear, and said, "We'd better go." We held hands as we skipped to the parking lot. I revved up Scarlett and cranked the heat. Amelia shivered in her seat and rubbed her mittened hands together.

I met her eyes. She smiled, bit her lip. I'd figured all along that I'd kiss her good night, at least to be nice, but now I just plain wanted it. I leaned close to her, brushed her hair away from her face, and shut my eyes for that moment of contact. Her lips were as soft and sweet as I'd imagined.

I didn't feel that same blast of electricity, of need, as I had with Rachel. If Rachel was dark chocolate ice cream with raspberry ripple and macadamia nuts, Amelia was vanilla bean—simpler, safer, but still satisfying. And she was here. I could have done this all night: our lips melting together, then pulling apart, tingling, over and over again. But we had only ten minutes to get Amelia home by curfew.

The porch light snapped on when we pulled up. Obviously, one or both of her parents were standing by the front door, watching. I cleared my throat. "Well. That was the best film on global warming I've ever seen."

Amelia giggled. "Does that mean you'd like to see it again sometime?"

"Sure. But do you think we could see one on recycling or strip mining instead? Just for variety."

Her smile shone in the dark. Its ghost glowed beside me all the way home.

**23**

*From the Rainbow Alliance Internet Lounge:*

**schmitty:** Well, I'd say the AVD was a roaring success.

**rachel_greenbean:** I couldn't agree more. Great job, everyone! I'm confident we've started a new tradition that will last for years to come. :-)

**writergrrl:** I agree . . . except you know what? I kind of hope it *doesn't* last. Because maybe that will mean society is so accepting of us—of *everyone*—that we don't need it anymore.

**z-dawg:** Yo, writergrrl, what is going on with

you and C??? I saw you dancing cheek 2 cheek!!!

**kittykat96:** I didn't even get to dance with Colby cuz she was w/you the whole time. *pouts*

**bananarama:** Yeah, are you two a Thing now or what?

**van_the_man:** Now now, don't be rude. Let the ladies have their privacy.

**van_the_man:** Sekritmessej to Amelia: TELL ME EVERYTHING!!!

**writergrrl:** You guys are terrible! I'm trying to look at the big picture here—the world and society and the future and stuff—and all you want is dirt.

**van_the_man:** God made dirt, so dirt don't hurt!

**z-dawg:** Come on, this brotha's starving 4 some romance.

**writergrrl:** As a certain friend of mine (*cough* Zak *cough*) would say, N to the O.

• • •

Van wrung all the juicy details from me as we rode to school Monday morning. As I talked, I felt my cheeks blush as red as Scarlett.

"What about you?" I asked. "You seemed to be getting plenty of play."

Van fidgeted, feet tapping, picking at his fingernails. "Well, there was this one guy from Gull Lake."

I grinned. "Yeah?"

"Yeah. Really cute and smart and all-around adorable? After you and Amelia took off, we danced, like, three songs in a row. Maybe it would've been more, but then his mom picked him up."

"Still, that's awesome! You get his info?"

Van slumped and looked out the window. "Not exactly."

"What!"

"After what happened on New Year's, I didn't have the nerve."

I groaned. "Vaaan! That was one guy. One jerky, totally-not-worth-it guy."

"I know."

"It's not too late. You could look him up online."

"I didn't even get his name. You'd have to, like, drive me to Gull Lake so we could stalk him."

"I'd do it, you know." I owed Van. All his nagging (or encouragement, whatever you wanted to call it) had paid off. I had the memory of Amelia's lips on mine to prove it.

He shook his head and hauled himself upright. "It

doesn't matter. We've got you taken care of. One out of two ain't bad."

We got our copies of the new *Watchman* during homeroom, and there were Mo and I, taking up half of page five. All morning people I didn't know walked up to me between classes, holding out their papers and asking, "Is this you? Did this really happen to your dog?" And acting impressed when I said yes.

I wasn't used to this, to people looking at me and thinking, *Wow, that Colby Bingham? She did something really great*. I wasn't used to people looking at me at all. Now I was suddenly in the spotlight (on page five, anyway), and for once I didn't get the feeling everyone was thinking, *Shrimp, slacker, lesbo*. They were thinking, *Dog rescuer*. Two of my teachers even called me a hero.

It was stupid—yet stupendous. Between the article and Amelia, I felt like a flashlight with fresh batteries, shining bright again. It almost made me feel like I could stand another year of high school.

On Tuesday red and pink balloons bobbed off lockers, smacking you in the face if you didn't watch out. Heart-shaped candy caked our molars in every class. The entire school buzzed with Valentine's Day drama. Everyone was hung up on whether so-and-so had bought them a flower from the student council sale, and whether that flower was a rose or a carnation, and whether it was red for true love, pink for crushes, or yellow for friendship.

Unfortunately, "everyone" included me. I actually laid down the cash for a pink rose for Amelia; I didn't want to get her hopes up—or mine. But I was relieved when I was called to the door during algebra to pick up a pink rose of my own, plus a yellow carnation from Van.

With Rachel, every moment had felt like a frayed wire, humming with energy, showering sparks when she touched me. Not that it wasn't exciting to be with Amelia, but it was more like a Ferris wheel, not a roller coaster. Maybe it was because I kept ordering myself to take things slow. The longer I held back, the longer things would last before she decided it was "too much" and cut me off.

I didn't kiss her again that whole week. Instead, we just talked—at school and at night by phone. We never seemed to run out of things to say to each other. Amelia made me feel like I could say anything. Or maybe it was just that after months of talking mostly to Van and Mo, I was overflowing with things to say. Anyway, it was so different from how I'd felt around Rachel, always afraid the next thing I said would show I was the world's biggest idiot.

"Aren't your parents suspicious?" I asked once.

"Don't they want to know why this random girl is calling you every day?"

"Promise you won't get mad? I told them there's a new phone tutoring program at school, and you're calling for help in math."

"What about your friends? What do you tell them?"

"Outside the Alliance? Math again."

"You know, you lie an awful lot for a good girl."

"I know," she said. "I know, and I hate it."

I wished I hadn't said anything. "It's only half a lie, anyway," I told her. "I'm terrible at math."

• • •

Friday night Robyn coached Mo and me on "leave it"—a command that was supposed to prevent Mo from picking up chicken bones, chipmunk carcasses, used Kleenexes, and other random garbage around Trail's End. But we were hopeless at it, thanks to my total lack of focus. I kept thinking about the next time I'd see Amelia.

Robyn said, "You seem a bit distracted, Colby."

I blushed. "Sorry. It's just, there's—things."

"It's okay. It's nice to see you looking so happy." Robyn scratched Mo's chest, and he flopped on his side for a belly rub. Lorraine and Oscar trotted up. Robyn did her best to pet all three dogs at once.

"I met this girl," I blurted, then mentally kicked myself. Weeks of keeping my private life private—*kaput*.

Not to mention I didn't know whether Robyn was okay with the gay thing—though, of course, if she had a problem with it, I'd grab Mo and leave without another word. I didn't have room in my life for that crap.

But Robyn grinned. "That's terrific! I wondered if that was it. That glow in your cheeks, that sparkle in your eye—it looked like love to me."

"Well, I don't know if I would go that far," I said.

"What's her name?"

"Amelia."

"And what's she like? What makes her special?"

I blushed even harder. "I don't know. She's— I don't know."

"But she's awesome, huh?" Robyn said.

"Yeah, pretty much."

Robyn stopped dog juggling and gave me a quick hug. "Well, congratulations, Colby. You deserve a nice girl."

"A nice girl," I repeated. "Who are you, my mother?"

The words just slipped out, and I felt a little jolt in my gut, like an elevator dropping two inches. I wanted to believe that Mom would like Amelia. I wanted to believe she'd be cheering for me, too. But I didn't know—and I never would.

I'd come close to telling her, once. It had been fall of freshman year. Mom was sick and getting sicker. Liliana, who I'd seen around school but had never spoken to much, had cornered me in the third-floor bathroom one afternoon. She snapped her watermelon gum and said, "You like girls, don't you?" Before I could answer or ask how she knew, she'd planted her mouth on mine and sucked my breath away. Then she turned and walked out, giving me a wink and a wave over her shoulder. I stood there so long that I was late to English.

There's a big difference between thinking you might be gay and actually doing something about it. Well, I guess Liliana had done it *for* me—but either way, a hypothetical had become a reality. I'd kissed a girl. And I'd liked it. And I wanted to do it again.

Over dinner Mom had teased, "Well, *somebody's* head is in the clouds. What's up, Bee?"

The dazed smile dropped from my face as I stared across the table at her—at her bruised-looking eyes and pale skin. She wore a tie-dyed scarf to keep her bald head warm, and her sweater hung loose across her gaunt shoulders. I think I knew that she wasn't going to get better. I knew it, and I thought, *If you wait long enough, you'll never have to tell her. You'll never have to risk her loving you any less.*

So I'd mumbled, "Nothing," and the moment passed. I had no idea then how many times I would regret that: hiding myself from the person I loved most.

But now, the word *mother* had an even stranger effect on Robyn. I could have sworn, as she stooped to give Lorraine another scratch, that there were tears in her eyes.

• • •

Later, I felt guilty for blabbing to Robyn about Amelia. Since Mom wasn't around, Dad should have been next to know—not Mo's freaking veterinarian. Van was right: I had to tell my father the truth. But what if coming out was the final straw that made Dad buy a rig—whatever color—and drive from sea to shining sea, never to return again?

Still, I wished I could tell him. Even when we spent the day under the same roof, I felt like we were each sealed in a crystal bubble. It looked so easy to reach out and touch each other, but there was only so close we'd get before—*crack!*—knocking each other back. Something kept us apart, kept us from talking about anything that mattered. Kept him from understanding how much I needed him.

Dad got in late that night. When I woke the next morning, I started working up the nerve to tell him. But while I was out jogging with Mo, I realized the timing was terrible. I had to be at work soon, and if it turned into some big discussion—as it no doubt would—I'd have to duck out in the middle. For eight hours, the two of us would be stuck stewing.

So when Dad asked, over breakfast, "What's news, Bee?" I said, "Nothing much. Same old, same old." I would tell him at dinner instead.

But when I came home that night, Dad was watching a special on TV about some tropical island where people wear nothing but paint, and the birds are so bright and fancy they look like something a kid drew with a whole box of Crayolas. I sat down to watch it with him, and we ate the Chinese takeout I'd picked up. Mo sat between us, drooling, before giving up and slumping onto the couch with a grunt. Soon Mo's eyelids drooped shut.

I couldn't possibly tell Dad now. We were too comfortable and relaxed. There'd been no talk of my grades or buying trucks. Why risk spoiling the little bit of happiness we had?

**24**

**THERE WAS NO** school on Monday because of Presidents' Day. I drove over to Amelia's to pick her up. She ran out to Scarlett, hair streaming behind her, and stuck her head in. "Can you come inside for a couple minutes? My mother wants to meet you."

I shut off the engine. "You're kidding."

"Unfortunately, no." Amelia made a face. "She said if I was going to spend so much time with you, it was good manners to introduce you. But they still don't, you know, *know*."

"Relax," I said. "I won't reveal the awful truth."

The Hoogendoorns' house was cheery and cozy—a bit too much, in my opinion. There was a grandfather clock in the front hall, flanked by the kind of oversize, glassy-eyed dolls that got animated by evil spirits and went on homicidal rampages in horror movies. There wasn't a flat surface that didn't have half a dozen "country charm" knickknacks on it.

Mrs. Hoogendoorn matched her house. She had a fluffy, bobbed haircut and wore a sweatshirt cross-stitched with daisies. I couldn't imagine my own mother wearing a shirt like that in a million years. "You must be Colby," she said. She shared Amelia's dimples. "We've heard so much about you and your puppy."

I stifled a smirk. "It's nice to meet you, too," I said in my best for-adults-only voice.

"It's so good to see Amelia branching out: making new friends, getting involved in the school community," Mrs. Hoogendoorn said as if Amelia weren't there and I was another parent. "Like her Ecology Club and the tutoring program. I've never seen her so happy."

"Yes," I agreed. "High school's a great time for expanding your horizons." I tried to catch Amelia's eye, daring her to keep a straight face, but she was intensely interested in straightening a row of ceramic roosters on the mantelpiece.

"Well, I'll let you girls get to whatever it is you've got planned. Amelia, please call if you won't be home in time for dinner." Mrs. Hoogendoorn saw us to the door and waved as we drove away.

The laughter we'd been struggling to contain burst out. We couldn't even talk until we were out on the main road. I wiped the tears from my eyes. "What is it we've got planned, anyway?"

"We could go to your place," Amelia suggested.

My imagination took over. I felt very warm all of a sudden. "Math tutoring?"

She smiled sweetly. "I left my calculator at home. Should we go back for it?"

"I'll share mine with you," I said, pulling up at a stoplight. "If you ask nicely."

Amelia leaned over and kissed me for the first time in a week. Her lips tasted like peppermint. "Was that nice enough?" she asked when the light turned green.

As if Scarlett and my brain ran on the same circuit, they both completely stalled out. I revved up the engine, and we lurched forward once more. "Very nice," I managed.

Mo was overjoyed to see Amelia again, and he got a whole lot more slobber on her. I was a little jealous, to be honest. We baked brownies and sat on the couch to eat them, straight out of the pan with a spoon. "Delicious," I said through a fudgy mouthful, passing the pan back to Amelia as Mo watched. "But not as delicious as you."

Amelia fumbled with the pan. "Likewise, I'm sure. I mean, I know I don't really have any basis for comparison, but you seem really, um, good at it."

"Making brownies?" I asked innocently. "I just follow the directions on the box."

"You know what I mean! How many girls have you kissed, anyway?"

"It's not the quantity, it's the quality," I teased, but her eyes were serious. She really wanted to know. "Just two," I said. "I mean, three. You—"

"And Rachel, right?"

I nodded.

"I thought so. Who else?"

"Liliana, a few times back in ninth grade, but you know what she's like. It's her life's mission to lock lips with every girl in school."

"I'm offended she hasn't kissed me yet."

I grinned. "Don't worry, it's only a matter of time."

"I'll be on my guard," Amelia said. "So, really? Rachel, Liliana, and me? That's it?"

"What's that supposed to mean?"

"Just, you always act so, I don't know, tough, like you've seen everything—"

"And done everyone?"

"Don't take it the wrong way," Amelia said. "I'm glad I'm only number three. I guess I just assumed— You're so comfortable with who you are, you know? Everyone knows about you, and you don't even care."

I shrugged. "After Liliana, the rumor mill started rolling. I didn't have much choice. Besides, I had bigger things to worry about."

"Like what?"

"My mom."

Amelia winced. "Oh. Of course. I'm sorry."

"It's okay." I didn't tell her that kissing Liliana had been the most effective way I had of forgetting Mom's cancer for a few minutes. I hadn't given a shit whether other kids found out about our make-out sessions or what they thought of me.

Amelia sighed and settled against me, pan in her lap. "When I figured out that I might be—you know—I thought about it for a really long time. I wanted to be sure it was true, I guess. I don't think I slept for a week. I thought about it all night, every night."

"How did you figure it out?"

"Oh, um—there was this girl last summer. At church camp. Nothing happened, but—well, I had some dreams. Not all of them while I was asleep."

"I know what that's like," I said. "My seventh-grade social studies teacher, Ms. Whittier? I once dreamed about shopping at Victoria's Secret with her. I didn't learn a thing about the imports and exports of Guatemala that year, but I memorized every freckle on her face."

We laughed.

"Your mom seemed really nice," I said.

"She *is* really nice. But trust me, Colby"—Amelia sat up and took another spoonful of brownie—"you can be a nice person and still get things dead wrong."

"I guess you're right."

"How'd you do it?" Amelia asked. "Break it to your dad, I mean?"

The brownies turned to concrete in my stomach. I forced out a little laugh. "Dad's away too much to be bothered by anything I do. Just catch your parents when they're feeling guilty about something. Trust me, they'll say okay to just about anything—even something like Mo. Right, buddy?"

Mo took this as an invitation to step forward at last, thrusting his snout at the brownie pan. Amelia hopped off the couch, holding the pan high. Mo did a charmingly awkward three-legged dance beside her into the kitchen, hoping for leftovers, but Amelia set the meager remains on top of the refrigerator, well out of his reach. Then she tumbled back onto the couch, and I pulled her against me, relieved to move onto an activity that didn't involve talking.

## 25

**O**N FRIDAY I was about to knock on Robyn's door but stopped with my knuckles half an inch from the wood. I could hear Lenny's gruff voice: ". . . don't like to see you working so hard."

Robyn murmured in response. Then—

"Of course it's work. It doesn't matter what you're wearing or whether you're drinking tea with crumpets. It's work. Look at you. You're exhausted."

Back to Robyn, who should have been a librarian, she talked so quietly.

"What I see is you running this business almost single-handedly—not to mention being sole breadwinner right now—and going way beyond what any sane person would do for a kid who, to put it kindly, sounds like she's got some issues. What am I missing?"

Robyn again.

"I hate to say it, but there are times when I'm truly glad we don't have kids. You already worry yourself sick over every stray you meet."

Then Lenny's voice dropped, leaving Mo and me with just the sound of traffic from Harrington Road and my chattering teeth. Mo whined at my side, wondering why we were still standing on the icy steps when dog biscuits and rubber postmen awaited us within. *"Shhh."* I stroked his ears and strained mine. Still nothing. Maybe they'd left the kitchen.

Robyn and Lenny were arguing about me, that much was clear. Part of me wanted to tiptoe down the stairs, climb into Scarlett, and never come back. I didn't know what was worse: being a charity case or being the kid that Robyn, for whatever reason, couldn't have. Suddenly, the eagerness seeping from her every invitation made so much sad sense. I hadn't wanted Robyn to pity me, but now I pitied her.

Still, who did Lenny think he was, bossing Robyn around? Where did he get off comparing me to a stray animal? Anger kept me on the doorstep. I counted to thirty, so they'd know I absolutely hadn't been standing there long enough to eavesdrop, then knocked.

Robyn answered, the usual scrabble-footed posse at

her heels. Were her eyes red? Was her smile a little too big? I wasn't sure. "Colby! Mo! I didn't hear you pull in."

I released Mo into the house and took off my coat. Lenny sat on one of the stools at the counter, watching silently. "How's it going?" he said before standing and adding, "I'll let you all get to it."

Robyn and I didn't dawdle over our tea, and the whole time we were working, I kept glancing down the hall toward that closed bedroom door. I left right afterward, making up an excuse about babysitting with Van. I appreciated what Robyn was doing for me, but I didn't want her to get the impression I couldn't walk away whenever I wanted.

• • •

Dad made blueberry pancakes on Sunday morning, fancier than normal. I should have known something was up, but I tucked in without a clue, savoring the tang of the berries on my tongue. Mo drooled beside me.

Then it happened. "I've got a lead on a rig," Dad said, mopping up the last drips of syrup on his plate with a dry wedge of pancake. "Reasonable price, outside of St. Louis. And pink!"

My stomach was on the verge of catapulting its contents back onto my plate. "What kind of pink?"

Dad sighed. "I don't know, Bee. Pink is pink."

"Pink is *not* pink. There are all different kinds. Baby pink. Flamingo pink. Fuchsia. Magenta." I sounded like a five-year-old.

Dad's voice rose. "You didn't specify which kind of pink when we made our agreement. I already told the lady I'd swing by to see it."

"When are you going?"

"Next time SwifTrux sends me that way. Could be this week, could be later."

I shut my eyes. It wasn't like life would get any worse after Dad bought the truck. It would just stretch on, as unchanging and endless as the gray asphalt and white lines zipping by under his tires, until he ran out of gas.

I could go all out, with the tears and fist slamming and swearing, make him promise to stay. If that didn't work, I could slit my wrists, then blame him from my cozy, white bed in the state hospital. I remembered my promise to Mom: to be strong, to help Dad however I could.

When I opened my eyes, Dad was watching me— waiting for me to give my blessing, I guess, although he'd practically put an offer on the truck already.

"Fine," I said. "Do what you want to do. Like always."

I spent the rest of the morning shut up in my room

and then hung out that afternoon at Amelia's house, trouncing her little brother, Neil, at gin rummy and trying to rouse his sleepy hamsters. Mrs. Hoogendoorn only popped her head in once to ask if maybe we should be spending more time with the math tutoring and less time "fiddling around."

It was weird being there, unable to touch Amelia. Obviously, I wasn't about to make out with her in front of Neil, but I felt her stiffen whenever my hand even brushed her knee. I had to keep reminding myself that it wasn't my fault, or hers. But whose was it?

When I pulled up at home that night, the Chevy was gone. Dad was probably at O'Duffy's, his favorite pub. I finished up my homework with the TV on, keeping half an eye out for headlights beaming through the living room window, but Dad still wasn't home by the time I crashed. I wanted to see him so badly—but only if he'd tell me he changed his mind.

The next morning I waited until I heard the telltale roar of Dad's rig before I let Mo out of my room. It was only when Dad pulled out of Trail's End that I realized I'd failed to tell him about Amelia and me yet again.

**I** N TYPICAL MICHIGAN fashion, March came in like a lamb: warm and soft, wet and smelly, as the neighbors' neglected dog shit began to defrost. March always fooled us into thinking spring was here, just before it roared out like a lion, leaving us all stunned and shivering in our boots. Still, for the first time in months, it wasn't completely dark at six p.m.—just dishwater gray.

The Westnedge High concert band performed early Sunday afternoon. I went to hear Amelia play. From the back of the auditorium, I watched her family sit front and center. Van and I headed as far to the side as we could. The more time I spent with the Hoogendoorns, the more awkward it was when they showered me with sweet words about my "puppy" or my algebra tutoring, clueless that I'd rounded second base with their daughter.

The band took the stage, and the houselights dimmed. Everyone in the band wore black pants or skirts with white shirts and blouses. They looked like waiters. I could barely pick out Amelia in the clarinet section; she'd told me she was first chair, but that meant precisely zip to me. Then, halfway through the show, the director announced that she'd be soloing in a jazz song called "Blue Shades."

When she stood, the other musicians faded into the darkness. It was like she'd put me under a spell. The song did nothing for me—give me catchy lyrics and a solid beat any day—but I stared, mouth hanging, in awe. Lips pursed around the mouthpiece of her clarinet, Amelia shut her eyes and notes poured out, one moment piping so high my ears tingled, the next burbling low in my gut. She looked as if she were in a trance herself.

When she sat down again, the auditorium exploded with applause. *That's my girlfriend!* I wanted to tell everyone. *That gorgeous, talented person chose me out of all the losers at this school.* I wished I'd thought to buy her flowers.

After the show, when the throngs of proud parents had dispersed, Van and I made our way to the band room.

Amelia introduced me to her friends in the group—she didn't call me her girlfriend, but I got the sense some people suspected—and then we all went to Fazoli's.

Van and I munched breadsticks as the band geeks dissected the performance. Amelia groaned that she slipped on tempo *twice* during her solo, but I said, "Don't be silly, you were incredible."

She beamed. "Really?"

I knew I'd said the perfect thing, for once.

Later, she squeezed into Scarlett between Van and me, her thigh right up against mine, slowly burning a hole through my jeans. We dropped off Van at his place, then doubled back to mine. Mo demanded a walk, so we strolled around Trail's End for a while, hand in hand. We didn't even let go when the Van Der Beek kids ambushed us. I wondered if any of my other neighbors were watching and almost hoped they were, hoped they could see the happiness on my face when Amelia smiled at me. And if they told Dad, well, that would take care of that.

Back inside, I heated a pan of milk on the stove for hot chocolate. "I look like a penguin," Amelia said. "I'm going to change." She slid into my bedroom with her backpack, and it took all my willpower not to follow her in there. I busied myself stirring every last clump of cocoa powder into the milk.

Amelia emerged wearing track pants and a sweat-shirt. "Much better," she said, stepping up behind me and brushing my hair aside to kiss the back of my neck. I put down my spoon, turned, and met her lips full-on. Some people might not have found Amelia's outfit sexy. But this was the first time I'd ever seen the shape of her legs not hidden under a skirt.

When we came up for air, Amelia gasped. "Who, exactly, said chocolate is better than sex?"

"It wasn't me, I swear." Amelia had said *sex*! "Great legs, by the way."

She looked down. "Really? You think so?"

"I know so." I poured the chocolate into two mugs: Tony the Tiger for me, South Haven sunset for Amelia. "I thought maybe wearing skirts was part of your religion or something. I mean, if it's your style, it's your style. But *damn*, you look good." My resolve to take things slowly was evaporating by the minute. I turned and slid my hands over her hips.

"Pants make my butt look enormous," she said.

"Pants make your butt look amazing."

We cuddled up on the couch and drank our hot chocolate. Mo wanted to nestle between us, but I banished him to the end of the couch, where he curled into a tiny—tiny for him, anyway—ball and fell asleep. Amelia set down her mug and leaned her head on my shoulder, which of course meant I had to set down my mug and stroke her peach-scented hair.

"Did you really like the concert?" she asked sleepily.

"It wasn't really my thing," I admitted. "But you were truly fantastic."

"I wasn't *fantastic*. But I was pretty good, wasn't I?" She took off her glasses and set them on the coffee table beside her mug, then settled closer, her face against my neck, her arms around my waist.

I wriggled down, side by side with her, and slid my hands just a little way under her sweatshirt, just enough to feel the silk of her skin under my fingertips. "Where are you right now?" I asked. "Band after-party? Documentary about factory farming? Bingo at the community center?"

"I'm just here. I'm tired of lying. If my parents figure it out, they figure it out. I kind of wish they would."

I waited for her to say more, but she didn't.

I listened to her breathing slow down, felt her heart beating so close to mine. My arm had fallen asleep, but I couldn't have cared less. "Are you sleeping?" I whispered.

"No. Just comfortable."

"Because we could go to bed. I mean, uh, to take a nap, if you want. There's more room."

"I don't need more room," Amelia said, "but sure. Let's move."

My heart went into triple time as I shut Mo out of the bedroom with a pat on the head as an apology. He whined for a few minutes before I heard a grunt and a thump and knew he'd resigned himself to the couch. But there was only so much thought I could give to Mo when Amelia was peeling up my shirt, unhooking my bra, putting her lips where no girl had put her lips before.

**27**

**T**HE SKY OUTSIDE my bedroom window was as soft and faded as an old pair of jeans. Amelia *had* fallen asleep, eventually, her hair fanned across my pillow. I watched her chest rise and fall, wondering how, in spite of all my screwups, I'd ended up with such a beautiful girl in my bed. So many times I'd dreamed of Rachel lying there, but this was better. Rachel had been a dream, a hopeless one. Amelia was real.

My alarm clock said it was almost seven. I hoped Amelia's parents hadn't expected her home for dinner. I'd ask her, but first I'd take Mo outside for a pit stop. Then I'd slide back into bed and wake her up much more nicely than she'd ever been woken up before.

I silently rolled off the mattress and picked through the jumble of clothes on the floor. As I pulled on my jeans, my cell phone plopped out of the pocket onto the carpet. I scooped it up and scanned the display's glowing silver letters: five missed calls. *Shit.* I'd turned off the ringer for Amelia's concert and forgotten to turn it back on.

I finished dressing and edged out of the bedroom, easing the door closed behind me. When I flipped open the phone, all the calls were from Dad. God, he was going to be pissed. Sure enough, as I skipped through each voice mail, he sounded more worried and angry than the time before. "Where the hell are you, Colby? You'd better have a damn good reason for not picking up that phone!"

I slumped onto the couch beside Mo, shut my eyes, and took a long breath before pressing my thumb to speed-dial Dad.

He jumped right in. "What the hell is going on? I've been calling every hour since two!"

"Dad. I'm really, really sorry. I went to this concert thing at school and forgot to turn the ringer back on."

"You could have been lying dead on the street for all I knew! I was all set to send Aunt Sue looking for you."

"I'm sorry. It was a mistake. It'll never happen again."

"Damn right it won't, or you'll be back at Sue's before you know what hit you."

"No, I won't."

"Excuse me, young lady? What did you say?"

I couldn't contain my own anger. "I said no! I'm seventeen. I've got a job. I'll get an apartment of my own. I'd move into a homeless shelter before going back to Aunt Sue's." Okay, maybe that was a bit too much. "You can't treat me like a grown-up one minute and a little kid the next! I told you I'm sorry. Maybe you'd rather I was dead."

The line went so quiet I wondered if he'd hurled his phone out the window. Then he said tightly, "You're right, Colby. I overreacted."

"Thank you!"

"I was worried. You're all I've got."

"I know. I'm sorry."

"I called to tell you I'll be home tonight—late. Don't wait up."

"Okay. I won't."

"Everything's all right where you are?"

"Everything's fine. I'm at home with Mo and— I'm at home with Mo."

I cursed myself for that stammer. I could practically see Dad's eyebrows drawing into a suspicious frown. "Bee, do you have someone over? A boy?"

"No, I don't have a boy over!" Never mind that Dad knew Van had been over hundreds of times while he was away. "I have a *friend* over. A female friend. Some of us like human contact occasionally. And I told you, I didn't hear the phone because the ringer was off. End of story."

"All right, all right. I'll let you get back to whatever you're up to."

*Whatever we're up to—ha!* I growled and threw my phone on the floor. Mo's head jerked up. He leapt off the couch to investigate, giving the phone a thorough sniffing over. I forced myself to take deep breaths. I wouldn't let Dad ruin my day—the closest thing to a perfect day that I'd known in so long.

My bedroom door squeaked, and there stood Amelia, fully dressed. I smiled weakly at her. "Why'd you have to go and put on all those clothes?"

She tipped her head to the side. "Just a friend?"

*Fuck.* "Not just a friend! Definitely not just a friend."

She picked up her glasses from the coffee table, automatically shining them on her shirt before slipping them back on. "He doesn't know, does he? He doesn't know about you."

"I've been meaning to tell him." I stared miserably down at my feet. My big toe poked out of the sock on my left foot.

"You didn't even tell him my name. Is that top secret, too?"

"God! Of course not, Amelia, but—"

"You acted like my parents not knowing was some

terrible thing. And this whole time you haven't even told your own father."

"It was wrong," I said. "I knew it was wrong to pressure you. I apologized, remember?"

"And the other week, when I asked you how you'd told him?"

"I never exactly said I'd told him," I muttered.

"Right. You just let me keep on believing you had. Huge difference." She walked to the door and pulled on her shoes. "Look, Colby. Unlike you, I don't have a problem going out with 'closet cases.' But what gave you the idea I like being *lied* to?"

I could have thrown myself at her feet and apologized. Explained why I hadn't told Dad. Promised to call him back, right that minute, and set the record straight (so to speak). Then we could have tumbled back into my bed and pretended this never happened.

But I stared into Amelia's sharp hazel eyes and saw Rachel pushing my hands away under the star-watching blanket. I saw Dad hugging me good-bye, slamming the door of his rig, pulling out of Trail's End week after week. I saw Mom lying frail and yellow as a handful of straw in her hospital bed, tubes sticking out all over her body, sleeping her way through our final hours together. I couldn't take it one more time. I couldn't let Amelia leave me, even if there was only one way to stop her: by leaving her first.

I shoved myself up from the couch. "Get your coat, and I'll drive you home. This is one liar you won't have to see ever again."

"Colby, I—"

"I mean it." My voice was quiet but harsh. "It's over. Get your coat."

We drove to Amelia's house in silence, and she didn't bother to wipe the tears streaming down her cheeks. When we arrived, she slammed the door and ran for the glow of her porch. I gunned the engine and went home, not bothering to make sure she got inside okay. Mo and I walked circles around Trail's End until my shoes were soaked with the last slush of winter and my feet burned with cold.

**28**

**I** **BARELY SLEPT** that night, but when Dad asked me at breakfast if everything was all right, I didn't bother telling the truth. What was the point? Just like Rachel, Amelia was over.

I trudged zombielike through school. Midterms were coming up. I thought I had a fair shot at some Bs—maybe even As in history and English. But algebra had me worried. Thanks to Amelia, I hadn't spent the usual amount of time going over my homework with Van. Too bad none of the time I'd spent with her had actually been math related. My algebra teacher, Mr. Yang, passed out a sheet with the list of topics we'd be tested on. Halfway down the list, my brain shut down.

After work, I locked myself in my bedroom and

called Van. "I'm throwing myself on your mercy. How do I graph a rational function again?"

"You have some nerve," he said, "thinking about algebra at a time like this."

"I don't know what—"

"Col, don't lie to me. I saw Amelia's face at school today. What did you do?"

"I didn't—"

"I just do not get you. This beautiful, sweet girl throws herself at you, and you blow her off—not once, but twice. I'd kill for what you had."

"She was about to dump me!"

"It was a preemptive dump?" Van's voice cracked. "You're making me sick. Do you know how much trouble I went to?"

"What the hell are you talking about?"

"Getting Michael to assign that *Watchman* article to Amelia. Convincing Amelia to ask you out. Making sure you didn't blow the whole thing before it got off the ground. But obviously, I shouldn't have bothered. You can be a real asshole, Colby, you know that?"

So that was why Van hadn't told me he knew Amelia from the Alliance. He'd known damn well I wouldn't want to be set up—not by him, and definitely not by my ex-almost-girlfriend's new boyfriend!

"I didn't ask you to play matchmaker," I snarled.

"Finding romance was *your* New Year's resolution, but have you done a damn thing about your own life? Have you taken one single step to hunt down that 'adorable' kid from Gull Lake? No, you're too busy controlling my life. 'Get over Rachel.' 'Go out with Amelia.' Why don't you mind your own business for once?"

"You're the one asking me for algebra help," Van said. "I'll tell you this: good luck. Good luck getting out of your own mess for a change."

• • •

At least the algebra midterm was multiple choice. I had clear-cut options instead of infinite ways to go wrong. I randomly shaded the answer bubbles on my test sheet, and, at the end of the period, Mr. Yang zapped it through the scoring machine. Thirty-two percent. Unless Van decided to forgive me, and soon, I could count on algebra joining my already bursting-with-fun summer schedule.

Oddly enough, what kept me going was the prospect of seeing Robyn on Friday night. We'd drink tea. We'd talk dog stuff. She'd listen. She'd care.

At five fifteen Mo and I showed up on her doorstep with fresh—well, fresh as anything from a tin—English tea biscuits I'd picked up at Meijer. Lenny's truck was parked outside, so I knew he'd be holed up in the bedroom, pretending to sleep or whatever he did when I was over. I hated the feeling that he was lurking just out of sight, watching the minutes tick by until I left.

Robyn answered the door, sweat suited and smiling. If it weren't for the cookies in one hand and the leash in the other, I might have thrown my arms around her, buried my face in her shoulder, and cried all my mistakes away. That was how desperate I felt.

Instead, I just smiled back.

"Come on in," she said. "I've already got the water on."

"What will we do when the weather gets warm?" I asked. "Too warm for tea, I mean?"

Robyn shooed Oscar, Lorraine, and Fontine, and they pranced backward into the kitchen. "I like a tall glass of lemonade. Or there's always iced tea," she said.

I pulled off my shoes and coat and unleashed Mo. The way he greeted the others, you'd think he hadn't seen them in years instead of the two hours since day care. "My mother used to make sun tea, let it brew in the kitchen window," I said. "I put so much sugar in mine, it might as well've been Kool-Aid." I hadn't thought of Mom's sun tea in ages. The memory flared just for a second before sputtering out into reality.

Robyn poured hot water into our teacups, and I picked out a cranberry tea bag. Plumes of red swirled as I dunked it.

"How was your week?" Robyn asked.

"Terrible. My algebra midterm bit me in the ass. I got an F."

"Oh, Colby. That's a shame. How'd that happen?"

I skipped the question. "On the bright side, I got an A in history."

"Can you get some tutoring, for the algebra? You're a smart girl—"

"It's not like anyone *uses* algebra. When's the last time you graphed a rational function?"

"Colby, you can't fail algebra. You owe it to yourself not to fail."

"I won't fail it! I just had a bad week, okay? Amelia and I—"

"Oh no." Robyn looked like I'd told her the president got shot. "She seemed like such a nice girl, from everything you told me."

"I know," I said. "You don't have to rub it in. Van's already done enough."

"You just seemed so happy."

The conversation was spiraling downward. Robyn was supposed to listen, nod, say it was too bad, and leave me alone. Not scold me. Not plan for the next time. Not ask me questions I didn't want to answer.

"You're not my mother," I muttered.

She blinked. "Excuse me?"

"I came here for help with Mo, not to get a lecture

on grades or dating or the rest of my shitty life!" My voice rose. "I know you want a kid and can't have one or whatever, but I'm not up for adoption, okay? I don't need a new mother, so stop trying to be her!"

The bedroom door creaked open, and Lenny's footsteps thudded through the house. He loomed in the kitchen doorway. "You've got some nerve, talking to Robyn that way."

"Len, it's okay," Robyn said. "She's just upset. She's had a tough week."

Lenny shook his head. "After all you've done for her, you shouldn't have to listen to this bullshit." He glared at me. "Robyn operated on your dog for free. She's given you free day care. Free obedience training. Free tea. And how do you repay her?"

"Lenny," Robyn said softly, putting a hand on his arm, "please. Let me handle this."

"You think your life is so tough," Lenny said, brushing her away. "So, you don't have a mother. Fine. You've still got a father, and from what I hear, he works his ass off to take care of you. You've got friends, a girlfriend. You have Robyn, who for whatever reason gives a damn about you. You have a house, a truck, school, a dog. But you act like it's all nothing. What the hell is wrong with you?"

"Lenny!" Robyn shouted. "That's enough!"

Lenny swung around and strode back to the bedroom. The whole house shook when he slammed the door, the wagging-dog clock on the wall knocked crooked.

"I'm so sorry, Colby," Robyn began. Her cheeks looked as pink and raw as canned salmon. "It's being laid off. And his own childhood was pretty tough. He didn't mean it."

I slid off my stool. I had to get out of there.

Lenny was right. Robyn plied me with tea instead of dog biscuits, conversation instead of pats, but when all was said and done, she treated me more like a stray dog than a kid—like one of those half-dead worms in her shoe box hospital.

I didn't need that.

I crammed my feet into my sneakers and threw my coat over my shoulder. I didn't bother leashing up Mo, just yanked open the door and called him to me. "Thanks for everything," I told Robyn, "but you can find some other sorry kid to take care of now."

• • •

When I thought things couldn't get any worse, Dad called. "This morning I dropped off a load in Jefferson City. I couldn't pass up the chance to check out that rig in St. Louis."

My throat tightened.

"It looked great," Dad continued. "Twelve years old, but well maintained. I'll take it for an inspection before I lay down any money, of course, but as of now it's looking like a go."

Words tried to wrestle free from my mouth but couldn't.

"It's pink—bubble gum pink. Lady who's selling it says it takes a real secure man to drive a pink rig." Dad laughed. "I'll try to remember that when the guys are giving me hell."

An "oh" escaped me like a sigh of wind. Mo pawed his way up on the couch beside me.

"I've still got to work out the financing. I'll visit the bank when I'm home next. And I've got to keep this whole O-O deal under wraps till the details are ironed out. The day I give SwifTrux my notice, we're going out to dinner. Somewhere nice this time."

To celebrate Dad leaving me for good. I picked at the frayed edge of Mo's collar, and he stared at me reproachfully. Why wasn't I using that hand to pet him?

"Bee? Is everything all right?"

I coughed, and words sprang free at last. "No problem," I croaked, as I'd said hundreds of times before. I blinked back tears. "No problem," I repeated. "Don't worry about me."

Why couldn't Dad hear that I didn't mean it?

**29**

**WHEN MOM DIED,** the whole inside of my body had throbbed with the pain. Now I felt dried out. Empty. Like there was nothing left to feel.

Sunday night when Mo got into some crud behind Mr. Harmon's trailer (I didn't want to think about what it might have been; all I knew was it was crunchy) and puked mightily two hours later, I silently cleaned it up and decided not to go to school the next day. It started as an excuse: I couldn't leave Mo alone when he was sick, could I? What if he got worse?

But even in the morning when Mo was his normal self again, I didn't go. School offered me nothing but six hours crammed in a desk, hoping my teachers wouldn't call on me. Between classes, no hallway or bathroom was safe; I could always run into Amelia or Van or Rachel or Michael or *somebody* who reminded me how much things sucked. At the rate I was going, I'd be twenty before I graduated. I wouldn't be going to college, no matter how much money Dad stuffed in my piggy bank.

That afternoon Dad called and wanted to know why I hadn't gone to school. The office had called him about my unexcused absence. I told him I'd been having "woman trouble," which usually got him off my case and did this time, too.

"You don't look all that bad," he said when he saw me the next morning as I made a great show of clutching my stomach and staggering to the bathroom first thing.

"Well, I *feel* bad. I think it's turning into the flu. Just let me take one more day off, please? So I'll be good as new tomorrow."

Dad sighed and called the school with my excuse. I prayed they wouldn't bring up my midterm grades. Dad was supposed to sign my progress report, but I figured I could put that off for at least another week; my guidance counselor knew Dad was away a lot.

No mention was made of my algebra grade. I was safe.

I didn't go back to school on Wednesday, either. Dad's voice, coming from south of Indianapolis after another call from the school office, was seriously pissed.

"Colby Alicia Bingham, what the hell has gotten into you? I am this close to calling Aunt Sue."

It was an empty threat, and we both knew it. I had money, I had wheels, and I had no desire to sleep on Aunt Sue's burnt-coffee-smelling couch. Dad was hundreds of miles away, driving farther every minute. There wasn't a thing he could do, short of setting the police on me. And he wouldn't do that as long as I kept answering my phone, proving I was alive and well.

Staying home from school meant I didn't have to worry about what to do with Mo all day now that Robyn was out of the picture. We slept late and spent the mornings lying on the couch watching the sports channel. When we went out, I'd catch Mr. Harmon spying on us from behind his curtains, no doubt convinced we were up to no good. Even the littler Van Der Beeks seemed suspicious that I wasn't in school, especially when I told them that, no, I hadn't actually skipped so I could have the pleasure of playing with them instead.

After lunch we would hop in Scarlett and drive to the nature preserve near West Lake. We walked among the skeletal trees until Mo's belly was caked with mud and burrs—not that he noticed. I tried to keep my brain as bare as the trees, but every now and again memories trickled through the cracks like melting snow. I saw my old soccer ball bouncing from my foot to Rachel's

222

and back, a conversation without words. Meals at our kitchen table with three places set, then two, then one. Amelia's smile after I kissed her the first time and her tears when I dumped her. One of Robyn's hands holding a teacup, the other stretching down with a dog biscuit. Van holding Teddy. Dad watching football. Mom fading away.

Van called, at first just once a day, then many times. I ignored his calls. His messages alternated between irritated and concerned. He came by my place and pounded on the door, jiggling the knob until I thought it would come off in his hand. Mo jumped, wagging and *woof*ing, wondering why I didn't open up.

"Colby, if you're trying to hide, you should close the curtains! I can see you."

What made Van think I was trying to hide? Just the same, I stood and drew the curtains, blocking out his gaping face. I didn't care if he saw me, but I didn't want to see *him*.

"I know you!" he shouted. "You can't live like a hermit forever. That's your dad's thing, remember? You're different. You need people. Besides, we need to talk. I'm really sor—"

I dug my mp3 player out of my desk, put my ear buds in, and lay on my bed, the music pulsing so loudly it hurt. I let ten songs play before I turned it off and sat up. I'd half expected Van to break a window and let himself in, but he hadn't. I stuck my head out the front door.

Nobody.

E-mails and texts piled up in my inboxes. Liliana offered to bring me chicken soup "or anything else you need ;-)." Rachel told me she could drop off my homework assignments. Zak sent me links to a dozen different videos featuring baby pandas, baby kittens, and baby humans, any of which would have made a normal person smile. Even Mr. Peabody e-mailed "just to check in." I didn't respond to any of it.

Dad, on the other hand, had stopped calling. Maybe he'd accepted that I was through with school for good, and he'd called to let them know. Hey, I could dream.

I was afraid Aunt Sue would eventually show up, but Dad must have kept my exploits to himself. If he admitted he couldn't keep me in line, she'd hold it over his head forever.

I felt a pang when five fifteen rolled around on Friday night, and Mo and I were home doing nothing. I knew Mo couldn't tell one day from another, but when he paced restlessly through every room before slumping to the carpet, I couldn't help wondering if he missed his date with Robyn, Oscar, Fontine, and Lorraine.

Saturday, I bagged groceries for eight hours straight

in full robot mode. I came home to find Mo had gotten into the garbage. So much time at home, out of my routine, had made me careless. I swept up the coffee grounds, apple cores, and shreds of tissue and lay on the couch, eyes fused shut. I was too tired even to watch TV.

• • •

Mo and I drove down to West Lake again Sunday morning, while the rest of town was either asleep or at church. We walked along the barren beach, not far from the spot where I'd spent my last night with Rachel. It was the first time I'd brought Mo to the water's edge, and he didn't seem sure what to make of it. He hopscotched back and forth along the snaking line where the water lapped the sand, his nose going wild. Whenever the breeze gave the water an extra shove up the shore, Mo leapt backward as if the lake were lava. Then he edged closer again, too intrigued to stay away. Wherever he'd come from, pre-Harrington Road, it clearly hadn't been near water.

"Where *did* you come from?" I asked him. "Were you a city dog or a country dog?"

I didn't think about Mo's previous life very often. He was such a friendly dog; people must have shown him some kindness. But there was the way he'd ended up, lost and gaunt, even before his close encounter of the four-wheeled kind. The way he flinched whenever

**225**

I picked up the broom. They say a dog always knows how to find its way home, so why was Mo running in the opposite direction?

Unless he wasn't. Unless I'd gotten it all wrong, and he'd been running toward home after all, and I'd merely been a distraction—a distraction that caused an accident, an amputation, and a sorry new life with a sorry new owner.

Maybe Mo belonged to a family down south, a mom and a dad and two little boys. And they'd been camping in the Upper Peninsula, and there was a big thunderstorm up in the hills—and Mo hid, the way he always did at loud noises—only afterward he got disoriented and trotted off in the wrong direction. After hours of searching, the family had to get back on the road home. Mo hit the road, too, because it was the only chance he had of seeing them again. Along the way he met other people, some kind, some cruel. But the whole time there was only one thing on his mind: getting home to that mom and dad and two little boys. And I'd stopped him.

The more I thought about it, the more real the story became. The little boys had names: Jonathan and Toby. Their parents were Miranda and Sam. They lived in a split-level down in Elkhart, Indiana, and they still had a food dish with Mo's name on it—except his name wasn't

Mo, it was Sparky—that they left on the back porch in case he showed up. At night the boys knelt by their beds—bunk beds, of course—and said their prayers, adding, "Please, God, help Sparky find his way home." Miranda kissed their tears away as she tucked them in.

It was ridiculous. It would have made the sappiest Sunday night movie ever. But I still had to drag a knuckle across my eyes as the lake and trees dissolved in a blur. What made me think Mo was better off now than he'd been before? What if the only thing that kept him with me was the leash clipped to his collar—the leash I never let go? I'd always believed the leash kept him safe. But maybe I was just as terrified he'd leave me as soon as he had the opportunity.

Sure, Mo looked happy, stalking along the beach, snuffling the sand. But what if he was simply making the best of a bad situation? Didn't he deserve the chance to do better than me?

"Mo," I said, but it was barely a whisper. I stopped walking. "Mo! Over here!"

Mo turned his head. When I squatted on the sand, he picked his way back toward me, leash drooping to the ground between us.

"You're a good dog," I said, and reached into the plush at his neck to unclip the leash from his collar.

He sat there, tail swishing up sand devils, head

cocked to one side, tongue out. He was waiting for an explanation. He thought it was a game.

"Go on," I told him. "You're free. You can leave if you want. I won't stop you."

He still didn't get the hint, so I stood up, shoving the leash into my coat pocket. He got to his feet, too. Then a rustle in the trees—a bird, a squirrel?—made his ears go up, and he whirled around and barreled down the beach away from me. He disappeared into the trees with a crash.

I stood watching the spot where he'd disappeared, straining my ears for the sound of snapping twigs, waiting for him to return.

But he didn't. Mo wasn't coming back.

I felt worse when I stopped thinking about myself for a minute and thought about Mo. What if he ended up on another dangerous road, lost another leg? What if he didn't make it this time? What if he starved to death before he got wherever he was going, or got mistaken for a coyote and shot? What if someone beat him and forced him into a cage, then threw him into the ring with a snarling pit bull?

Maybe I couldn't give him a perfect life, the life he dreamed about when he was asleep and his feet started twitching and his tail thumped against the carpet and he gave excited little yips. But it was better than a lot of the alternatives. And I had let him loose. I was so stupid!

I picked my way through the woods, shouting Mo's name, then stopping to listen for him tearing through the undergrowth. I walked on and on until I was nearly lost and my voice was hoarse from shouting. Luckily, I found my way to the lakeshore and followed it back to the empty beach before I became one of those people you read about who live for months in the woods surviving on acorns and raw squirrel.

When I couldn't shout anymore, I sat on the sand and began to cry. The rest of the world became so muffled that I didn't hear the patter of feet. Then Mo started licking the tears off my face.

**30**

*From the Rainbow Alliance Internet Lounge:*

> **yinyang:** Anyone else stuck here over spring break and want to hang out?
>
> **schmitty:** Sorry, Rachel and I are going on a trip with the JCC.
>
> **rachel_greenbean:** We leave tomorrow morning for DC. We're going to the White House, the Holocaust Museum, and everything!
>
> **j0ck25:** @yinyang, I'll be around if you want to shoot some hoops or something.
>
> **stonebutterfly:** I'm going to watch all 7 seasons of Buffy the Vampire Slayer. Y'all

are welcome to join me.

**kittykat96:** I'm going shopping for a new bathing suit AND I'm going to get my hair cut AND I'm getting my first mani-pedi of the year!!! You could come too.

**yinyang:** Looks like I've got all kinds of options. :-)

**z-dawg:** Anyone know what's up with C? She wasn't at school all week and never answered my messages. Know anything, V?

**van_the_man:** That girl is a riddle wrapped in a mystery inside an enigma covered in rusty barbed wire.

**van_the_man:** In other words, not really.

**kittykat96:** Maybe you should ask Amelia.

**writergrrl:** I've never seen Buffy. What time are you starting, Stone?

• • •

I woke the next morning to Mo jumping from bed to floor. Bacon. I smelled bacon frying. What day was it? Dad wasn't due home until Tuesday night. Was it really Wednesday? Could two days have passed without my noticing?

Mo whined and pawed at my bedroom door. I groggily followed him into the living room. Dad glanced over from the stove, where, along with the bacon, he had slices of bread soaking in a pan of egg and milk. "Morning, Bee." Mo sat beside him and began drooling.

"What day is it?" I croaked.

"Monday."

"But you're not supposed—"

"No. But that was before you went and skipped a whole week of school, and Van called me, all in a panic, saying you wouldn't answer his calls or open the door for anything. He actually called SwifTrux to get my number, you know that? That boy's been your best friend for years. I know you don't like school too much, but you love *him*."

My stomach turned, and it wasn't just the smell of too much grease early in the morning. Of course Van had been worried. Of course he'd called Dad. I *was* an asshole.

"I called the dispatch," Dad said. "Told them I had a family emergency. I had to drive bobtail all the way home from Atlanta, and believe me, Colby, that did not make me happy. So there better be a good explanation for this mess. What have you been doing all this time?"

"Nothing. Working. Taking care of Mo."

"I meant what I said about Aunt Sue."

"So did I. I won't go, Dad."

We stared at each other, arms folded across our

chests, jaws set. Amelia said I was the spitting image of Mom, but she hadn't seen Dad and me butt heads.

Dad turned back to the stove, flipping the bacon onto a plate. Mo stared, a mustache of drool dangling from his lips. "Go and get dressed," Dad said. "We'll continue this conversation over breakfast."

I took Mo out for a couple of laps around Trail's End. It was still early. The other trailers glowed dimly. Now that the days were longer than the nights again, I could see where we were going. I didn't have to worry about stepping in someone else's dog shit or tripping over a Big Wheel. We took our time, Mo lifting his nose to sniff the almost-warm currents of air.

What did Dad honestly think he could do to me?

As we plowed through our French toast, Dad started in. "A mental health day here and there is one thing, but you can't take whole weeks off from school. The school doesn't like it, and neither do I. You're seventeen years old, plenty old enough to take responsibility—"

"Wait, Dad." He did, fork poised above his plate. Syrup dripped in a thin line. "You're always talking about what I need to do. What about what *you* need to do?"

He dropped the fork with a clatter. "What *I* need to do is be out there driving that truck, earning a living to keep a roof over your head and food on your plate."

"Why do you bother? If I'm old enough to 'take responsibility,' why don't you let me do that? If I starve, I starve."

"Maybe I'm not the best father out there, but I'm not going to leave you to fend for yourself."

I shoved my plate away and stood. Mo clambered to his feet. "Can't you see?" I said. "You already have. I don't care about insurance benefits or college funds. I'd rather have no father at all than a half-assed one like you." I pulled Mo's leash from the doorknob. "Come on, Mo."

Dad was standing now. "Colby Alicia Bingham! Don't you dare walk out on me."

"Why not? You do it to me, every single week." I pulled on my coat and grabbed my wallet and keys. "Mom asked me to help you out, but I can't do it anymore. I'm sick of it."

My hands shook as I turned the key in Scarlett's ignition. We started driving. It didn't matter where.

• • •

When we returned after a few hours of aimless wandering through the nature preserve, the old Chevy was nowhere in sight. Mo was so worn out, he flopped onto the couch and barely noticed when I ate a peanut butter sandwich three feet away.

I waited for Dad to walk in the door and pick up

where we'd left off, but he hadn't returned by the time I left for work. After my shift at Meijer, the car was still gone, although I couldn't swear Dad hadn't been home in between. I went to bed, saying good night to no one but Mo, just like usual.

It was still pitch-black when my bedroom door swung open. I sat up, heart pounding. Mo stumbled off the bed, shaking himself. There was a figure in the doorway, silhouetted by the living-room lights.

"Up," Dad said. "Now."

My eyes darted to the alarm clock. Four a.m. "What's going on?"

"Get up and get dressed, or I'll make you. And you won't like it."

I rolled out of bed and pulled on my clothes, my sleep-starved brain struggling to process what was going on. If Dad had been a different person, I might have thought he was hauling me out of bed to give me a beating. As it was, I was coming up empty. "What's going on?" I repeated, staggering into the living room, rubbing my puffy eyes. "It's spring break."

"Not for you it isn't. Go and wash up. Then pack a bag with some clothes, your personal things."

"I'm not going to Aunt Sue's!"

"Who said anything about Aunt Sue's? Go pack your bag. You'll want your pillow and quilt, too. Your butt had better be back in this room and ready to go in ten minutes."

I splashed water on my raccoon eyes and dragged a brush through my hair. I stuffed my backpack with an extra pair of jeans, a bunch of underwear and socks and T-shirts, some sweatshirts, my toothbrush and shampoo, and my mp3 player.

I hoped Dad wasn't sending me off to some kind of wilderness intervention camp.

"What about Mo?" I asked.

"He's packed." Dad nodded to a couple of Meijer bags by the door. Mo's dishes and chew toys stuck out of the tops.

"What about breakfast?"

"We'll deal with that later. I'll take out your things; you take Mo to do his thing. Then we're hitting the road."

*Hitting the road.* So that was it. Dad wasn't hauling me off to wilderness camp or a home for wayward girls. He was taking me with him in his rig. Once upon a time, the idea of riding side by side with Dad for a whole week, seeing the country, would have thrilled me. Now it sounded like a prison sentence. I wondered if it was too late to stay with Aunt Sue after all.

Mo made a production of sniffing the entire inside of Dad's rig: the huge bucket seats, the dozens of buttons and dials and compartments, the litter bag hanging from the center console, the cave of a "bedroom" behind the seats where Dad spent most of his nights. I buckled myself in. Dad punched in his security code, turned the key, and the engine roared to life, a zillion times louder than Scarlett. We circled out of Trail's End and onto Harrington Road, heading for the freeway.

Dad said, "SwifTrux has a load for me to take from the Irish to Gay Bay."

"It's early, Dad. Try that again in English?"

"Sorry, Bee. That's South Bend to San Francisco."

"But what about *my* work?"

"Give me your manager's number. I'll call and explain things."

"I could lose my job over this."

"I doubt it. But if you do—well, you're young. You can find another."

"Does SwifTrux know you're doing this? Taking me with you?"

"Yep. I went to the local office yesterday and got written permission. Family emergency."

"What about Mo?"

"Dogs are allowed anytime. I know a guy who's got three." Dad reached back to give Mo a scratch. "Before you got Mo, I always thought a dog was more hassle than it's worth. But now that I know what a good pal he's been to you, I've been thinking maybe when I buy that truck, I'll buy myself a dog to go with it."

"Great," I muttered. "Get yourself another daughter, and you'll have two complete sets—one at home, one for the road."

"What was that?" Dad asked. The farther we drove, the more cheerful he sounded.

"Nothing." I scowled into the darkness.

**WE STOPPED AT** Burger King, where we didn't see Elvis but Dad bought us hash browns and French toast sticks. I crawled behind the seats and let Mo sit up front to take in the scenery, such as it was: bare orchards, barren fields, and withered vineyards in the early-morning light.

I slept most of the way to South Bend. After I woke I lay still, listening to the drone of the road beneath me, rocking with each curve and dip in the road. Had Dad told Aunt Sue his grand plan? What about Van? The roaming was sucking juice from my phone's battery faster than you could say "Rescue me." Seconds after I texted Van to assure him I wasn't dead, the screen went gray.

The truth was, I was excited to go to San Francisco. My family had always done most of its traveling within a few hours' drive: Chicago, Cedar Point, Mackinac Island. Twice we all flew down to Florida to visit Grammy and Pop-Pop; we went to the beach and to Disney World. But that had been years ago.

In South Bend we pulled off the freeway so Dad could pick up his load of pork rinds or tampons or whatever it was that Californians simply couldn't do without. I took Mo for a pit stop as Dad fussed with hitching up the trailer to the tractor. The air smelled wet and rotten, and we quickly climbed back in.

When Dad rejoined us, he pulled a little notebook from the driver door's storage compartment: his logbook, where he kept careful track of his mileage, hours, loads, and destinations. He jotted down the details and tucked the book away, then started up the engine once more. We pulled onto I-80, the long, white trailer extending behind us like a Lego block.

Dad talked with other drivers on his CB, usually boring stuff about traffic and state troopers, and I had a discussion with Mo about why he couldn't sit in the front seat at the same time as me. Dad and I didn't say much to each other.

Lots of drivers kept a TV in their "bedrooms." Not Dad. He didn't even have a laptop, even though almost every truck stop we passed advertised free Internet. Aside from his mattress, microwave, and mini-fridge, he just had a big stack of books back there. The battery in my mp3 player ran out way too soon, so I messed around with the FM. Every time I found a station that played decent music, we were out of range ten minutes later. It seemed like country was the only music that came in loud and clear, so I resigned myself to the twang.

When Dad had logged what felt like a hundred hours, he pulled into a motel just off the freeway in Middle-of-Nowhere, Iowa. "Don't get used to this motel business," he said. "It's just because this is your first night, I want you to be comfortable."

Ha. If Dad wanted me to be comfortable, he'd have left me at home.

We ordered a pizza and ate it sitting cross-legged on the bed, ESPN on the TV. After a while Dad stood up and took his toothbrush from his travel case. "I'd better hit the sack."

"It's eight o'clock," I said.

"Yep, and we'll be hitting the road again bright and early tomorrow. I'm setting the alarm for three thirty—okay?"

"What am I supposed to do now? I'm not even tired."

Dad shrugged. "Watch TV. Walk Mo. Read the Bible. Just be ready to go at four."

He stripped down to his T-shirt and shorts, pulled a sleep mask over his eyes, put in his ear plugs, and slid between the sheets. Soon he was snoring away. Mo climbed up on the bed beside him and joined in. Just great.

I perched on the corner of the bed and watched TV until my brain turned to pudding. I'd barely fallen asleep when Dad shook me and pulled me back out to the truck.

• • •

Later that morning Dad switched off the radio, silencing a mournful slide guitar and Toby Keith's crooning. "I guess you and me've got some talking to do. I know it's not something we're good at, but it's time we tried a little harder."

I stared out the window. Nebraska along Route 80 looked a lot like Iowa, which looked a lot like Illinois, which looked a lot like Indiana. They were all even more boring than southwest Michigan, something I hadn't thought possible. So much for seeing the country.

"I'm not saying we have to jump into anything heavy. We could start with the easy stuff, just catching up. I feel like we've been too busy fighting lately even to do that."

Mo let out a groan from where he lay sacked out behind us as if to say *I'm staying out of this one.*

"Fine," I said. "What do you want to talk about?"

"Well, forget school for now. How about your friends: Van, Rachel. You still hang out with her?"

I hadn't realized Dad ever *knew* I had a friend named Rachel, much less remembered her name. I must have mentioned her ages ago. "Not really," I muttered. "She has a boyfriend."

"Oh." Dad drummed his thumbs on the steering wheel. "That's like a full-time job for some kids, isn't it? What about you, Bee? You got a boyfriend?"

He was trying for casual, but it was utterly unconvincing. Obviously, he thought my meltdown was the result of some kind of boy trouble. I'd been dumped, or there was some boy I mooned over who wouldn't look at me twice. Some everyday girly teen drama.

I could lie or change the subject, the way I always did. But maybe because I was stuck on an endless freeway in endless empty fields, I suddenly couldn't stand to be trapped in another lie.

I sighed. "I'm gay."

There was a long moment of quiet, interrupted only by the squawk of voices on the CB. Dad reached over and thumbed down the volume. I waited for him to say *Not another word, Colby Alicia Bingham. What would your mother think if she were here?*

It was so quiet, I heard Dad breathe in through his nose before saying "That's all right, Bee. That's just fine." And he reached across the gap between us and gave my knee a little squeeze and a shake.

"Seriously?" I said. "You're seriously okay with it?"

Dad ran his hand over his bald spot. "Well, I guess, if I'm being honest, it wouldn't be my first choice for you. Life's got complications enough without—without something like that."

"It's not like I can help it," I said.

"I believe that, too. But even if you could help it"— he shot me a stern look—"it wouldn't stop me from loving you. It wouldn't change you being my daughter. You got that, Bee?"

I swallowed. "Got it."

There was another long silence, and then Dad drummed his fingers again. "Do you want to tell me about it?"

So much for not getting into the heavy stuff. I fidgeted with the cuffs of my sleeves. "What do you want to know?"

"Well, if it's not prying too much, I guess I'd like to know how it—how you—"

I wasn't about to tell Dad about my Victoria's Secret dream starring Ms. Whittier, my initiation by Liliana, my hopeless affair with Rachel, or my latest disaster with Amelia. "How'd *you* figure out you liked girls?" I countered.

He stared out into the vast, gray-blue sky, cocking his head like Mo. "I never thought about it," he admitted. "Never had to. It just came naturally. Pretty girl smiled at me, I smiled back."

"Well, it came naturally to me, too. Except it took a while to figure out what it meant."

"But how do you know it's not just—"

"A phase?" I nearly spat the words. "It's not, Dad. Trust me. It's permanent."

"Don't bite my head off, Bee. You've had however long to think about this, and I've had the last five minutes. Give me a break."

"Sorry."

Dad cleared his throat. "So. You got a girlfriend?"

"No. Not now." *Not ever.*

He patted my knee again. "You're young. In the meantime, I guess I don't have to worry about you running around with boys, huh?"

"Not so much."

"That's a relief." Dad hesitated. "Is Van—"

"Yeah," I said. "He's my 'good buddy.'"

Dad smiled wryly. "Put my foot in my mouth with that one, huh? I guess in the back of my head I already knew. I never worried about you being alone with him. You two were always more like sister and brother than anything else."

I waited for Dad to ask another question, but he didn't. It was almost funny. Even when we were talking, we weren't talking. Or was it that we'd already said everything that needed to be said? Except . . .

"Mom," I said. "Do you think she— I mean, if she'd known, would she—"

"Your mother always said you were no sheep but a lone wolf."

"What does that mean?"

"It means," Dad said, "she was always proud of you for doing things your own way. For being different. The only thing was, she hoped you'd find someone to run with one day. The problem with lone wolves is they get lonely." He glanced over at me. "Does that answer your question?"

"Yeah. I guess so."

I remembered how Mom had teased me the day I kissed Liliana. Had she suspected the truth then? Or was she simply happy to see *me* happy, whatever the reason?

Maybe it didn't matter. Either way, she'd loved me.

Dad turned the CB back up. "I've got to keep an ear out," he apologized. "You want the radio?"

"No," I said, "that's all right."

Who needed the radio? My heart beat in rhythm with the road.

**32**

**T**HE FARMLAND gave way to sweeps of brown earth, patchy with low, gray-green shrubs and lingering snow. If I strained my eyes, I could see smoky, purple peaks at the horizon.

"Welcome to Wyoming," Dad said.

"Is it just me or is most of this country just open space?" I asked.

"They say that if you took every person in the entire world and had them living all together, they'd fit in a space the size of Texas. So, yep, I guess it is." Dad grinned. "But there's plenty of pronghorn antelope and mule deer living here. Keep your eye out."

We stopped in late afternoon and spent the night at a near-deserted truck stop. Dad wanted me to take the "bedroom" and he'd sleep up front, but I refused. I was wide-awake.

The night air was chill and sharp and quiet. I helped Mo clamber onto a picnic table at the edge of the parking lot and lay beside him, my arm around his furry furnace of a body. Above us, the stars were so dense there was almost more light than darkness. I thought of stargazing with Rachel, but the stars had never been so bright as they looked here, hundreds of miles from what I'd call civilization, without anything to distract me.

Did Dad ever lie out and watch the stars? Did he wonder if Mom was out there, looking back at him? Did he worry what she'd think of his life now?

When it got too cold, Mo and I returned to the truck. Mo wuffled his way to Dad, curling against him with a grunt. I put my seat back and shut my eyes, not really caring if I slept. I let my thoughts approach as smoothly and silently as headlights in the rearview mirror, then glide past.

I wondered what Van was up to. Probably babysitting, or maybe skateboarding downtown until the cops came to enforce the curfew. And Amelia—probably asleep already, her dark hair fanned across her pillow, her glasses folded neatly on her bedside table. I felt a dull ache in my stomach. She hadn't deserved what I'd done.

Eventually, I must have fallen asleep, because Dad

was turning the key in the ignition, and we pulled out of the truck stop. The roads grew hillier, and the engine chugged as Dad pressed the accelerator all the way to the floor. We still weren't anywhere near the speed limit. We passed ranch land: cattle, horses, even bison. In the first light of morning I saw the promised pronghorns, with black-striped faces and forked antlers, bounding across the terrain. Mule deer stood still and wide-eyed, their tall ears splayed like donkeys'.

As we approached the Utah state line, the sage-covered hills gave way to rich, red-orange cliffs. I was exhausted but didn't want to miss a thing. I stared out the window as we rounded the Great Salt Lake and entered the Great Salt Desert, a table of white dust stretching to the horizon. Signs warned drivers that the next gas station was dozens of miles away. I was glad Dad had fueled up outside Salt Lake City; this didn't look like a place you'd want to be stranded.

Our third night we spent in Nevada. I let Dad persuade me to lie down in back with Mo, where I fell asleep before I knew it—but I was wide-awake when his alarm went off at three thirty, ready for a breakfast of granola bars and bananas. My body was getting used to Dad Standard Time.

We climbed out of the nubby, brown corduroy hills of Nevada into the frosty, evergreen-covered Sierra

Nevadas. Then we snaked back down, Dad riding the brake, me gripping the door handle. I wasn't used to roads this narrow, steep, or curvy—and this was a freeway!

"Feeling carsick?" Dad asked, and rolled down the window. I rolled mine down, too, and breathed in fresh, piney mountain air. Mo climbed onto my lap and stuck his snout out of the window, drinking it in.

The closer we got to the coast, the more the land smoothed out. Palm trees towered by the sides of the freeway, and brilliant pink flowers spilled over the median. Dad said they were bougainvillea; I didn't realize he knew a thing about flowers. What else had I missed in all our years apart?

I tracked our progress on Dad's beat-up road atlas, my finger edging over to that expanse of blue ink off to the left: the Pacific Ocean. I couldn't believe that after three and a half days of driving, we'd gone from Middle America to the edge of the world.

• • •

The San Francisco warehouse where Dad dropped off his cargo was in a stinky, ugly industrial area that could have been back in South Bend if it weren't for the telltale palm trees waving overhead.

"What now?" I asked as he filled out his log.

He shrugged. "Turn around and go back."

"You're kidding," I said. "We just got here!"

"SwifTrux has me picking up another load about an hour away in Vacaville, dropping off all the way back in Benton Harbor. There's always something that needs to go somewhere."

"Dad, listen. We just drove a zillion miles to get here, and now you're saying you want to turn around and leave without even seeing it?"

"It's not a matter of want, Bee. It's just my job. I do my sightseeing from the windows of my rig."

"What about me, then? I've never been to California before. Can't we at least stop for a couple hours and see the ocean? The Golden Gate Bridge? Something?"

Dad stared at his watch and chewed his lip. I put on my most pleading, pretty-please-with-a-cherry-on-top face. He sighed. "All right."

We couldn't abandon Mo, which meant driving or walking—no cable cars for us. Dad refused to drive on any hills in the city—it was illegal with the rig—so we took a not-very-scenic freeway until we saw the on-ramp for the Golden Gate Bridge. Dad pulled off and parked, and the three of us covered the rest of the distance on foot.

The Golden Gate was not what I'd expected. I'd pictured something more like McDonald's Golden Arches—you know, something that was actually golden.

The bridge was the same brilliant color as the cliffs where Wyoming met Utah, striking against the deep blue of the ocean beyond, the pale blue of the sky above. The cables dipped and rose like a graph in math class, and I thought of Van, wishing he were here to see it, too.

Dad and I waited patiently as Mo hobbled beside us up the long, zigzagging flight of stairs to the walkway. Mo didn't seem too sure about leaving solid ground so far below, but he liked the idea of being left behind even less.

Up on the bridge, the wind whipped around us so fiercely that it felt like we'd be blown off if it weren't for the railing. To our left was the Pacific Ocean, stretching out forever blue, speckled white with tiny boats in the distance. To our right was San Francisco Bay, with spring green hills beyond it. Ahead, more green headlands, and behind, over our right shoulders, downtown San Francisco, pale and spiky.

"That's Alcatraz," Dad said, cupping one hand around his mouth to be heard over the wind, pointing the other toward an island in the bay not far away. "Former home of Al Capone."

"Long swim to shore," I said.

"Exactly."

Even though I was shivering—who would have thought you'd need a winter coat in a place with palm trees?—I didn't want to turn back. Turning back meant climbing into the truck and heading home, where my mistakes were waiting for me.

"Let's go all the way across," I shouted. "I want to see the city from the other side."

It was a long walk—a really freaking long bridge—but after more than three days of being cooped up, the stretch felt good. We kept passing tourists posing for photos with Alcatraz and downtown San Francisco as the backdrop. Once they had their photo op, they turned around and scuttled back off the bridge to shelter. I spotted a pair of women holding hands, then a pair of men pushing a baby carriage. *Gay Bay.* I felt a twinge of envy; maybe coming out would have been easier if my family had lived here. I checked Dad's reaction to the couples, but either he hadn't noticed or he was pretending not to care.

On the other side we climbed down off the bridge and walked to the observation point. I picked a bench facing the city and sat, Mo panting at my feet. Dad eased down beside me and swiped his sweaty forehead with the back of his hand. "So. What do you think?" he asked.

"I don't know," I said. "I mean, it looks great and all—but how can I really tell? It's like I'm looking at a postcard. A 3-D postcard."

"With fifty-mile-an-hour winds," Dad said. We laughed.

"Don't you get tired of it? Always skipping from place to place, never stopping to *experience* things?"

Dad rubbed his chin. "I do, sometimes. But it's like I feel lighter when I'm moving, you know? When I stay too long in one spot, it's like there are weights dragging me down."

I wasn't sure I wanted the answer, but I asked anyway: "Am I one of those weights?"

"Bee! Never! It's not you. It's everything else. After your mother—"

"I miss Mom, too, you know."

"I know you do," Dad said. "Of course you do. It's hard. Harder than I ever imagined."

"The reason you never want to be home—is it because I remind you of Mom?"

"It isn't that I never want to be home—"

"Just answer the question! Is it?"

"You remind me of your mother in many ways," Dad said. "The way you're so fierce but also so loving. The way you found that damn dog and wouldn't give him up, wouldn't let him die. Wouldn't take no for an answer."

"But is that why you never come home?"

"I *do* want to come home. Never think I don't, Bee. All I think of, all week, is coming home again."

"I don't believe you. Then why would you leave in the first place? Do you have a girlfriend somewhere? Is that it?"

"What the—no! I do this because it's my job, Colby. It's how I take care of us."

"Bullshit!" A bunch of tourists heard me and swiveled their heads, but I didn't care. "Bullshit. Maybe you couldn't go back to driving a cab, but you didn't have to choose this. You don't have to keep doing OTR. You don't have to buy a rig of your own. Can't you see? It doesn't do any good to put away money for my college. I'm not going. I'm tired of school. I'm tired of everything. I'm tired of being alone. I'm tired of being a lone wolf, Dad."

Mo whined up at me. I wiped my stinging eyes. It was a long, cold walk back across the bridge.

**33**

**D**AD HAD LOST what I'd come to think of as his "driving smile." As we drove across California, he frowned at the road ahead. I slumped in my seat and took in the scenery. The pale green sweep of the Central Valley gathered itself into wrinkles and folds and towering, pine-covered mountains once more.

That night, taking in the fresh air at a Nevada truck stop, I watched the stars glow stronger in the purpling dusk. "It's so beautiful," I said, the words just slipping out. "I want to come back here someday—to all these places—and visit for real."

"If that's what you want," Dad said, "I don't doubt you'll find a way to do it."

"Not if I'm bagging groceries for the rest of my life. But hey—I could bag my way around the whole world, I bet."

"No daughter of mine is going to spend her life as a bagger," Dad said. "You're going to college."

"Not when I'm failing chemistry. And algebra," I added guiltily.

I waited for him to launch into another lecture, but he just stared out at the darkening hills. "I've decided something, Bee," he said. "I'm coming home."

His face was in shadow. I couldn't read his expression.

"I've talked so much about the future: getting you through college, buying a decent house someday. But tho present is what's most important. *You're* what's most important. I've let you down."

I wanted to tell him that it was all right. Except what he said was true. He *had* let me down. And everything *wasn't* all right. I let him keep talking.

"You've always seemed so strong, Bee—it didn't seem to matter whether I came or went; you always carried on. But maybe that's just what I wanted to see." He paused. "Truth is, I'm sick of being a lone wolf, too. When your mom died, I wasn't just sad—I was scared. The idea of starting over with a new company, maybe even a whole new career, terrified me. When I made the switch from cabdriving to trucking, your mom was there to help me through. But once she was gone, it seemed easier to go back to what I knew."

"*I* was still there," I said. "*I* could have helped you."

"I know, Bee. I know better now. And I'm sorry."

"What about that rig you're buying? What about your loan?"

"You know, this stuff with you distracted me. I never made it to the bank." I thought I heard a grin in Dad's voice. "I'll apply for some short-haul jobs near home, see what comes of that. If that doesn't work out, I'll think of something else. Until you finish high school, anyway."

It should have been the happiest news I'd heard in years, but I couldn't crack a smile. I was afraid that after another three days on the road, Dad would change his mind again.

I said, "That could take a while at the rate I'm going."

"You'll finish," Dad said. "You take as much time as you need to do it right. I'll be there."

He stood and slung an arm around my shoulder. And for the moment I believed him.

• • •

Driving back across the Great Salt Desert, so white and barren it might as well have been Antarctica, I started feeling homesick. I didn't look forward to returning to school and catching up on a whole week's worth of work, or going back to Meijer to bag groceries and mop bathrooms for hours on end (although I wouldn't mind collecting my paycheck). But I missed Van, who always meant well even when he stuck his nose where it didn't belong. I missed Robyn, who'd been awfully good to me. And I missed Amelia. Sure, I missed kissing her, feeling her skin against mine, but most of all I missed how comfortable I'd been around her. I'd never had to be anyone but myself.

I felt a nauseating wave of guilt every time I remembered her face when I dumped her. She'd wanted to tell me off, not break things off. I saw that now. I remembered Robyn saying how if she and Lenny gave up whenever things got hard, they'd never have made it so long. I'd done just that.

Dad glanced over at me as I plucked at the hem of my jeans, snapping off one frayed thread at a time. "Why so glum, Bee?"

"You know how you asked, the other day, if I have a girlfriend?"

"Yeah?"

"Well, I did," I said. "She was great. Her name was Amelia."

"So, what happened?"

I shook my head. "All you really need to know is, I screwed up."

"Oh." Dad chewed his lip. "Well, have you apologized?"

"I've thought about it," I said. "But even if I apologize, it's not like I deserve another chance."

"That's up to her, isn't it?" Dad said. "You apologize; she forgives. Or not."

"But it isn't fair."

"What isn't fair? You made a mistake. Everyone does."

"I know." I took a deep breath. "It's just, why should I keep getting second chances—with Amelia, with chemistry, with *anything*—when Mom never did? She got pregnant, dropped out of college, got disowned by her parents, got cancer, and died. And she was a good person. A great mother. Mo gets hit by a car, and all he loses is a leg. And he's just a dog! Where was Mom's second chance?"

Hearing his name, Mo stuck his head out of the back and cautiously licked my ear, then decided he needed to climb onto my lap. I hunched over his warm body, burying my face in his ruff. My throat swelled up like a cantaloupe, and tears ran in hot, salty streams into my mouth.

And Dad didn't say a thing to comfort me. Not one damn thing. He just kept driving.

Then I felt the truck slowing. My teeth knocked together as we jittered off the asphalt and onto the gravel of an emergency pull off. Dad put the truck in park and switched off the CB. And he still said nothing.

He reached down and tugged at my arms, unwinding them from Mo. I turned my head away, hair falling forward so he couldn't see my face as he pulled me from my seat. Mo scuttled out of the way, and I banged my knee on the gearshift, but I didn't have the strength to fight. Dad pulled me onto his lap, and I slumped against him, the steering wheel digging into my side, my face mashed against his flannel shirt as he wrapped his arms around me and cradled me, rocked me, saying, *"Shhh. Shhh. Shhh."*

I don't know how long we sat like that, but I ran out of tears and started breathing normally again and noticed how disgusting my nose was and began wishing I had a Kleenex. I sat up and rubbed my sleeves across my eyes and nose.

"You okay?" Dad asked awkwardly.

I nodded and began to slide off his lap, but he held me firm.

"Look, Bee. I've got something to say, and this might

be the only time I get the nerve to say it, so you better listen up. Got it?"

I nodded again, eyes squeezed shut in case I didn't like what I heard.

"Your mom, God bless her, *was* a good person, and I miss her every day, all the time. But you're not giving her near enough credit. Yeah, she got cancer. That sucks, and it sucks a whole lot more that she didn't make it. But the other things you mentioned—getting pregnant, dropping out—you make it sound like those were mistakes that ruined the rest of her life. And it's not true, Bee. It's not true."

I snuffled a particularly gross snuffle, and Dad leaned around me, fumbling behind the seat for the box of tissues. He tore one free, and I blew my nose twice, three times. Dad took the soggy mess from me and dropped it in the litterbag.

"Maybe it was an accident she met me in the first place, and maybe it was an accident we got together and made you. But your mother had a choice, Bee. She could've gone back to her folks and done everything they wanted her to. She could've gotten an abortion or given you up for adoption and pretended the whole thing never happened. In my opinion, that's what the real mistake would've been: living life their way instead of hers. But she didn't. She stayed with me and had you and raised you until—well, you know. You want to talk about second chances, Bee? You *were* her second chance."

I wanted to deny it, to point out what a stupid idea it was that I could be anyone's shot at redemption. But then I thought of Mo, as big a surprise for me as I was for my parents, and how things had changed since he came along. Not always for the better, but I'd never trade my life now for my life before I met him.

"I'm going to take a nap," I said, pulling away from Dad and crawling behind the seats.

Mo, who'd been watching us anxiously from the passenger seat, crept in beside me. I stroked his velvety ears and shut my eyes as we rolled back onto I-80, gathering speed again.

• • •

When I woke up, we were climbing into the mountains of northeast Utah, fiery cliffs closing in on us from either side. I moved up front. "Marigolds," I said.

"Hmm, Bee?" Dad asked, nudging the CB down a notch.

"Third grade, when my whole class grew marigolds in Dixie cups to give our moms on Mother's Day. Mine was so shrimpy and wilted, it wouldn't even grow a bud. It died two days after I gave it to Mom."

"I remember that," Dad said. "She thought it was sweet, how broken up you were."

"Yeah. I was a crybaby. But she just hugged me and kissed me, and you know what she said? That no flower in its right mind would be happy in a Dixie cup."

"She went out and bought a trowel and a packet of seeds," Dad said. "You two planted a whole patch of marigolds outside the front stoop."

"Red, gold, orange," I said. "They looked like flames. They lasted all summer long."

"I remember the time you and Mom stayed up half the night baking a birthday cake for me, so it'd be fresh when I got in from a marathon job."

"I remember that! Four in the morning, and we were eating pot roast and chocolate cake."

"That's right," Dad said. "I'd forgotten the pot roast. I just remember the two of you had flour all over your shirts. And you had chocolate all over your face, Bee, a chocolate mustache and beard."

"The neighbors must've thought we were crazy singing 'Happy Birthday' in the middle of the night like that."

"Well," Dad said, "it wasn't a problem till the candles set off the smoke alarm."

We laughed, hard.

"Do you remember," I said, "the time we all went smelt fishing, out by South Haven? And it poured all night, but we stayed out, anyway?"

"I do," Dad said. "I do."

The memories came thicker and faster, like a rainstorm unleashed from the sky, as the truck strained upward into the Rockies. We talked until we had to stop for the night.

**34**

**D**AD LET ME juice up my phone on his charger, and outside Cheyenne, I called Van from atop a beat-up picnic table while Dad refueled. "How do you catch a unique rabbit?" I asked.

"Colby, where are you?"

"Answer the question."

"You 'neak up on it, duh. Where the hell are you?"

"Wyoming. It's so beautiful. You should see it. There are mountains all around—well, Dad says they're not all mountains—some are only hills—but they're mountains compared to back home."

"I've just spent spring break changing Teddy's diapers and skating at the same old parks and parking lots, while you're off seeing the country without me."

"Only what I can see from the windows. But maybe someday we can see it together. Take a big road trip after graduation or something. I've really missed you."

"Me, too." Van coughed. "Say, uh, I don't suppose you've heard from Amelia?"

I groaned. "I've got three voice mails from her, but I skipped past them. I'm too scared."

"She's been calling me all week, asking if I've heard anything from you."

"Why? I mean, why does she give a rat's ass about me?"

"Hell if I know, the way you treated her."

"I know. I was awful."

"Yeah, you were. But at least you admit it. That's more than you can say about some people."

"Thanks a lot, Van."

"It's always my pleasure."

"No, I mean it. Thank you. Thanks for always trying to pull my head out of my ass. Thanks for telling me when I'm being a jerk. Thanks for, you know, just being there for me."

"Except with algebra."

"About that. Think you could help me get through the next quarter?"

"I think so," Van said. "But you gotta do something for me in exchange. Uh, remember that guy from Gull Lake?"

"Yeah? You ready to stake him out?"

"Nope, don't need to. I was skating downtown on the mall and saw him shopping—with his mother, I might add—and went for it."

"Seriously?"

"Seriously. I admit it, Colby. I'm a gutless little twerp. There's a reason I'd rather set you up, you know? I'm sorry about that, by the way. The whole Amelia thing. I shouldn't have—"

"It's okay," I said. "Really. Tell me about Mr. Adorable."

"Okay, well, I skated over, praying he'd remember me."

"And?"

"And he did! He gave me his number and screen name and everything."

I shook my head, grinning. "Unbelievable. And what about his mother?"

"What about her? She smiled and said 'Pleased to meet you' and all that. She knows about Trevin—that's his name, isn't it beautiful?—and she's totally okay with it."

"I told my dad," I said.

"You did? Holy shit, how'd that go?"

"It went okay. Better than I expected. But Van—it doesn't really sound like you need me for anything."

"*Au contraire,*" Van said. "I need you to babysit Teddy next Saturday."

"What?"

"God, Col, don't freak out. You'll get paid. That's another thing: after Mrs. Van Der Beek hired me to watch her kids—"

"What?"

"Yeah, it was one of those times I came by last week when you wouldn't open the door. She stepped outside in her bathrobe and slippers and said she'd seen me with Teddy and was I interested in sitting for her kids sometime."

"Those holy terrors?"

"I think they're cute," Van said. "Anyway, now that I've got a decent source of income, I can support my new lifestyle."

"So are you saying Saturday you're—"

I could practically see Van's smug, chip-toothed smile. "Yep. Donovan McIneany's going out on the town. Dinner and a movie, my friend."

"And he's not going to give you a hard time over being straight edge?"

"Nope. He's as clean as they come. Need I remind you, he was shopping with his *mother*?"

**269**

"Good point," I said.

Dad waved to me. He was ready to hit the road.

"I've got to go," I said. "But this is great news. I'm really happy for you! There's just one thing that worries me."

His voice went tense. "What?"

"Does Trevin know you've got the corniest sense of humor in the universe?"

There was a pause, and I felt bad for teasing him. He'd waited so long for this. Then he said, "You remember that Milk Dud joke? The one about the cow?"

"Unfortunately. Why?"

"I told it to him, and he laughed," Van said triumphantly. "Trevin laughed!"

• • •

Amelia's voice mails all went the same way: "Colby? It's Amelia again. Could you, um, call me when you get a chance? I really feel like we should talk. Um, okay, bye."

I didn't want to talk over the phone. I owed her an apology, big-time. I'd ring her doorbell. Look her in the eye. I'd even bring her flowers, except I didn't think I could pass it off in a way that wouldn't freak out her folks.

We pulled into Trail's End at dusk. I jogged a couple of laps with Mo and gave him a late dinner. He was overjoyed to be home. He trotted through each room, sniffing every speck of dust that had settled in the past week, making sure everything was as he'd left it. Dad stretched and gave a yawn worthy of Mo. "Want to order a pizza, Bee?"

"No thanks, I've got something I need to do. I'll be back in an hour or so."

"I might go to O'Duffy's, if that's all right with you."

"It's all right with me." I'd just spent what felt like a year's worth of time with Dad. We'd run out of things to say. In a good way. And if he kept his promise, we were going to see much more of each other in the year to come. One more night apart was nothing.

I showered, changed, and brushed my teeth. I wasn't getting any ideas, but it had been a couple of days since my last truck stop shower, and I was feeling grungy. I grabbed my keys and said good-bye to Dad and Mo.

Mrs. Hoogendoorn answered the door. Today her sweatshirt featured an embroidered cat lying in a bed of violets. Her eyes flicked to the grandfather clock in the hall, but she put on a cheery smile. "Colby."

Did she wonder where I'd been the past few weeks after spending so much time with her daughter? How had Amelia explained my sudden absence? What terrible things did Mrs. Hoogendoorn think of me now?

"I'm sorry to come by so late." Not that eight thirty was late in my version of reality, but it couldn't hurt to be on my best behavior. "Is Amelia here?"

Amelia was already pushing past her mother. In that first glimpse, the full weight of my stupidity fell on me. Her long hair swished past her shoulders, her cheeks were roses, and even though I was afraid what was coming wouldn't be pretty, I still lit up inside.

"Come on," she said, not quite meeting my eyes. "Let's go to my room."

I shucked off my shoes and followed her. She closed her bedroom door behind us and sat on the edge of her bed. I stood by the door.

"You may as well take off your coat and sit down," she said.

I did, sitting far enough away that her mattress wouldn't tip us toward each other. "Hi," I said. And then, before I could chicken out, "I'm sorry."

Amelia looked down at her hands. She was wearing the same paisley skirt as the day I met her. She looked just as flushed and nervous, too. "You hurt me, Colby."

"I know. And I'm really sorry. I wish I could promise never to do it again, but it would probably be a lie. I'm pretty much hopeless."

"That day when we—I was angry. Really angry. But

that didn't mean I—"

"I know," I said again. "I know that now."

"I've been thinking about telling my parents." Amelia's voice grew hushed. "I mean, when we were together, I thought about it all the time. But then after— I thought, 'What's the point?'"

"Believe me, I know how that goes." I lay back against Amelia's bedspread and stared at the ceiling: the tulip-shaped light, the tiny crack in the paint running from the light toward the corner of the room. "I told my dad, by the way."

"About you?"

"About us."

She smiled and lay beside me, so close our arms almost touched. "How'd he take it?"

"He took it fine. Just one more reason I deserve the Asshole of the Year Award."

"You couldn't know how he'd react. You were scared. You were protecting yourself."

"And you're way nicer than I ever deserved." I wanted to reach for Amelia's hand, to feel her fingers close around mine, but I didn't dare. I kept my eyes firmly on the ceiling. "Look, Amelia, I want another chance. I don't mean things have to go back to how they were. I mean, I'd like to try and be friends. I want to see you in the hall at school and say hi and know you don't hate my guts."

"I miss Mo."

"You do?"

"Thinking I'd never see Mo again made everything even worse."

"It hardly seems fair to keep the two of you apart on account of me."

"You think I could have visitation rights, is that what you're saying?"

I smiled. "Yeah. Have your people call my people. We'll work something out."

I heard a creak in the hallway and wondered if her mother was out there eavesdropping, but Amelia didn't seem to notice.

"Colby," she said, "is it stupid of me to want to start over?"

"It wouldn't really be starting over," I pointed out. "I blew that. It'd be starting from here."

"Even so. You know what I mean." She turned her face toward me, regarding me carefully from behind her glasses.

"I've missed you," I said.

Amelia rolled onto her side, propped up on one elbow. Her hair brushed my hand. I reached out, rubbed the silky strands between my fingers. "I've missed you, too," she said.

"More than Mo?"

"Well, I don't know about that."

I couldn't tell if she was teasing. I dropped my hand to my side.

"It took you three weeks to decide to apologize."

"I know."

"So I want three weeks, too." She bit her lip. "I need time to figure out how I feel about you after everything that's happened."

It wasn't the answer I wanted to hear. I wanted Amelia to roll on top of me and kiss me so hard I felt my insides explode. I wanted to slide my hands over her hair, her face, as her hands went up my shirt. But it wasn't going to happen. Not today.

I took her hand. She wrapped her fingers tightly around mine. I stood up, and our fingers slowly slid apart.

"I'll put it on my calendar," I said.

**35**

**"DO I HAVE** to go to school?" I asked Dad the next morning over scrambled eggs and toast, rubbing my bloodshot eyes. "What's one more day?"

Our trip to California and back had been a full seven-day run. Now it was Tuesday, and my classmates had already returned from spring break.

"You're going," Dad said. "Look, Bee. When the time comes, if you don't want to go to college, that's your decision. I'll respect it. I'd like you to go—your mom would have liked you to go—but I understand life might take you other places. Until then: school. I meant it about not being a bagger for the rest of your life. Remember that marigold. A Dixie cup isn't enough."

Dad sent me off with a note vaguely describing a family emergency. Still, my teachers didn't waste much sympathy on me, piling on homework for the week I'd missed. Mr. Yang looked especially skeptical of my excuse, but I kept my mouth shut and my eyes down as I copied his algebra assignments into my notebook. Hopefully, Van could help me catch up.

There was an Alliance meeting after school on Wednesday, and though I hadn't gone in months, I knew it was time to go back. At the end of the day I stepped tentatively into Mr. Peabody's room. With supernatural speed, he whipped around and said, "*Colby* Bingham! Where have you been?"

Amelia looked up, and I gave her a small, crooked smile and a shrug. Liliana ran up, threw her arms around me, and planted a kiss on my cheek. Zak high-fived me and said, "Welcome back, girlfriend." And just in case anyone had missed it, Van called, "Heeeeey, everyone, look who's here!" I could have throttled him.

But I wasn't there to hide. I sat in the circle next to Van and didn't budge, even when I saw Rachel making her way over.

"Colby, hi," she said. And in spite of everything, I felt a twinge. Maybe there was no getting over Rachel Greenstein, not completely. I'd given her my heart so

277

easily. Taking it back was much harder.

But maybe that's how it was supposed to be. I said, "Hey, Rachel. What have I missed?"

She looked surprised by my interest. I guess I couldn't blame her. "Well, um, National Day of Silence is coming up," she said. "And we've been talking about doing something for the talent show. Liliana wants us to sing 'Born This Way,' but Mr. P.'s pushing for 'True Colors.' And there's prom, and the end-of-year party, and Pride—"

"Great," I interrupted. "Count me in. For all of it."

• • •

I knew that whether or not Dad found a short-haul job, he was going to be OTR trucking for a while longer yet. I envisioned a future of chewed-up furniture and clawed-up curtains unless I made day care plans for Mo, but that wasn't the only reason I wanted to make things right with Robyn. I remembered what Amelia had said about rescued animals being eternally grateful to the people who saved them. I still wasn't convinced. I think somewhere down the line, everyone forgets the awful circumstances that brought them together, and at that point there's no pity or gratitude left. It's nothing more or less than plain old love.

The day Robyn saved Mo, she saved me, too. Robyn

and I weren't exactly friends, weren't exactly family—
we were just us. And I needed her.

On Friday I parked Scarlett in the clinic's lot. It
was later than usual, and the rooms in front of Robyn's
place were dark. Slowly, Mo and I climbed the wooden
stairs. I held my fist against the door but didn't knock.
Mo whined, and I reached down to stroke his ears, but I
still couldn't bring myself to knock. Van and Amelia had
been so forgiving. What if Robyn wasn't?

Mo couldn't take it anymore. He barked. I saw
the kitchen light go on. Lenny opened the door, Oscar,
Lorraine, and Fontine crowding around his legs. Mo
yanked on his leash so hard he broke free and charged
inside, jumping and licking and circling the other dogs
in the most enthusiastic reunion ever.

I was all set to run away and leave Mo there before
Lenny could open his mouth and chew me out for
daring to show my ungrateful face at Robyn's doorstep.
But instead he regarded me quietly. For the first time
I wondered if he had been another of Robyn's strays.
Maybe we weren't so different.

"Hey," I said.

"Hey," Lenny replied. He was wearing a gray shirt
with an orange and white name tag pinned to the chest.

"New job?" I asked. "Congratulations."

Lenny nodded. "Thanks. It'll do for now."

We stood a moment in silence. Then he said, "I'll get Robyn." He stepped back inside, calling, "Honey, there's someone here to see you!"

Robyn bustled past the dogs to the doorway. Her face lit up. "Colby, what a surprise. What a *nice* surprise."

"Sorry for coming so late," I said.

"Not at all. Come in out of the cold."

I stepped up to slide past her into the kitchen. But her arms caught me, wrapped around me, and pulled me tight. There was only one thing I could do: put my arms around her, too.

She finally let go of me and stepped back. "Take off your coat," she said. "I'll put the water on for tea."

• • •

### *From the Rainbow Alliance Internet Lounge:*

> **van_the_man:** Did everyone see the forecast for next weekend? 65 DEGREES!!! Spring is here!!!
>
> **kittykat96:** OMG YES! I am so lying out in my new bikini.
>
> **colb33:** Van and I are going to Milham Park to play soccer on Sunday. Feel free to join us.

**van_the_man:** Plus you'll get to meet my very special guest: the one . . . the only . . . TREVIN!!!

**z-dawg:** Can you go a freaking minute without talking about your new bf?

**van_the_man:** No. :-)

**j0ck25:** You know I'm there. Just name the time and place.

**colb33:** Cool, anyone else? My dad has this idea that I'm quitting my job to play soccer this summer, and I am so out of shape.

**writergrrl:** Does it sound awful that I don't even know how to play?

**van_the_man:** Don't worry your pretty little head. It would be our honor to teach you.

**colb33:** Totally . . . if you're up for it.

**writergrrl:** Will I have to wear pants?

**colb33:** It would help.

**writergrrl:** You ask a lot of a girl, Colby Bingham.

**colb33:** Some things never change.

**van_the_man:** AHEM. Sorry to interrupt this intimate exchange, but to confirm: Sunday at 2. Be there with bells on.

**van_the_man:** And pants.

**van_the_man:** Or just bells, but I'm pretty sure that's illegal in this state.

**writergrrl:** Could someone give me a ride?

**van_the_man:** Trevin will be escorting moi. But I know someone with a red pickup truck.

**writergrrl:** Colby?

**colb33:** Sure thing, I'll pick you up. It'll make Mo's day.